Blue
is for

John Fulghum Mysteries
Vol. III

Murder

E. W. Farnsworth

Blue Is for

Murder

John Fulghum Mysteries Vol. III

E. W. Farnsworth

ZIMBELL HOUSE PUBLISHING, LLC
Union Lake MI
2017

For permission requests, write to the publisher at the address below:
"Attention: Permissions Coordinator"
Zimbell House Publishing, LLC
PO Box 1172
Union Lake, Michigan 48387
mail to: info@zimbellhousepublishing.com

© 2017 E. W. Farnsworth
Book and Cover Design by The Book Planners
http://www.TheBookPlanner.com

Published in the United States by Zimbell House Publishing
http://www.ZimbellHousePublishing.com
All Rights Reserved

Print ISBN: 978-1-945967-03-0
Kindle ISBN: 978-1-94596-04-7
Digital ISBN: 978-1-954967-18-4
Trade Paper ISBN: 978-1-945967-36-8
Library of Congress Control Number: 2016960492

First Edition: January/2017
10 9 8 7 6 5 4

Dedication

Rita

Contents

Foreword

"Theodor Gottlieb Ursinus (1749–1800), a high-ranking Prussian civil servant and justice official, was poisoned by his wife Charlotte Ursinus (1760–1836). At the time, his death was ruled a stroke, but soon after the widow was found to have poisoned, between 1797 and 1801, not only her husband, but also her aunt and her lover, as well as to have attempted to poison her servant in 1803. Her sensational trial led to the first reliable method of identifying arsenic poisoning." — Wikipedia article on Arsenic Poisoning

There was a king reigned in the East;
There, when kings will sit to feast,
They get their fill before they think
With poisoned meat and poisoned drink.
He gathered all that springs to birth
From the many-venomed earth;
First a little, thence to more,
He sampled all her killing store;
And easy, smiling, seasoned sound,
Sate the king when healths went round.
They put arsenic in his meat
And stared aghast to watch him eat;
They poured strychnine in his cup
And shook to see him drink it up:
They shook, they stared as white's their shirt:
Them it was their poison hurt.
-I tell the tale that I heard told.
Mithridates, he died old.

-A. E. Housman, "Terence, this is stupid stuff," A Shropshire Lad 1896

Chapter 1

The Sayak Solution

In ancient Korea, and particularly in Joseon Dynasty, arsenic-sulfur compounds have been used as a major ingredient of sayak, which was a poison cocktail used in capital punishment of high-profile political figures and members of the royal family. Due to social and political prominence of the condemned, many of these events were well-documented, often in the Annals of Joseon Dynasty. — https://en.wikipedia.org/wiki/Arsenic_poisoning

John Fulghum, Private Investigator, was stopping at the Dunkin' Donuts on the way to his office as he always did when he first heard the news of Judge Stephen Anderson's death on WBZ News Radio. Suffering from a splitting headache, courtesy of a late night meeting with his old friend Jack Daniels, he was more worried about the meaning of "regular, regular" in the context of his morning coffee than the unsurprising demise of a centenarian Boston blue-blood in a secluded mansion near Pittsfield, Massachusetts.

"Good morning, Mr. Fulghum! Will that be 'regular, regular' like usual?"

The detective scowled and said gruffly, "Why are you always so gleeful at this god-awful hour of the morning?"

The server's face fell. Fulghum felt like a heel. It was a gray, melancholy day. He did not like being gratuitously unpleasant, especially with a young man who showed promise.

"Forget that. It was a long night, and I've got a hangover. Give me a regular, with two extra shots, Bennie." He held up a ten-dollar bill as a peace offering.

"You got it." Perking right up, Bennie grabbed a cup and began shoveling the sugar, flooding the sugar with cream, and then pouring the coffee with enough room for the extra shots. He was holding the first extra over the cup when he asked, "Did you hear about old man Anderson being murdered? It's all over the radio this morning." He handed Fulghum the coffee with a stir stick and napkins. In return, he received the ten-dollar bill that included his generous tip.

"Thanks, Mr. Fulghum." He made the change and ostentatiously dropped the bill and coins in his tip cup by the window. "The tip will go right into my college savings account, like always."

"Bennie, have you ever thought of joining the US Army?" Fulghum asked. As a former Special Forces officer and war hero, he knew both the advantages and drawbacks of military service.

The server shook his head pursing his lips as if he had heard that distant call before. He smiled affably and waited patiently for his best tipper to move right along. As an afterthought, he added, "When I think about that old geezer living like a hermit in an old haunted house in Pittsfield, I get the chills. Whoever killed him probably was doing God's work. Geez, he was over a hundred years old. I hope I don't live that long."

"'Mithridates, he died old,' Bennie."

"Mithra who?" The young man was nonplussed and scratched his head before replacing his Red Sox ball cap.

Fulghum sipped the coffee before he left the drive-in window to check that it passed muster. He nodded approvingly without another word to Bennie as he put it in his cup holder and drove away. A block away his headache eased off, and his memory kicked in. He stopped to pick up the Boston Globe and the Daily Racing Form. He scanned the headlines in the newspaper and read the article, "Judge Stephen Anderson, life-long Boston native." He shrugged and sighed.

Instead of proceeding to his office, he lit up a Marlboro and drove into the city to visit the Boston Globe archives. He smoked three more as he fought the morning traffic and edged his way through rush hour traffic into Bean City.

Fulghum was a Netizen, but he still relied on old forms throughout the day. According to the masthead of his favorite rag, The Daily Racing Form was "America's Turf Authority Since 1894." His preferred news source, the Boston Globe, was founded by a man named Charles H. Taylor in 1872. Fulghum knew that not everything in print would be transferred to the World Wide Web in searchable ways. Metadata was only a kind of shorthand that filtered out a lot of essential data. Old newspapers provide a treasure trove for the professional sleuth with a special connection to an insider at the papers. Besides, the archivist at the Globe was his old friend and sometime lover, Silvia Blackwood.

To her beautiful face buried in the print documents she was searching on her desk, he called out, "What's good about this morning, my buxom hard-boiled archivist?"

Sylvia looked up from her research and smiled. Formidable and obdurate to everyone else, she melted when she saw Fulghum walk into her office. She rose from the cushion on her captain's chair and sidled around her enormous, cluttered desk to hug the detective. He stood at attention like a wooden toy soldier while she pulled him close into her arms. She stood back and held him at arm's length while she examined him closely.

"You're a sourpuss today, I see. Fulghum, did you get out of bed on the wrong side?"

He gave her his crooked, ironical smile and said, "Figlear, Darcy. I'm not amused."

Silvia got a guilty look as she gazed down at her feet and shook her head. She went back to her chair mumbling, "I knew I'd pay for that."

She sat back and appraised Fulghum for a reaction. Her hand reached out instinctively for her ashtray, but she withdrew it immediately. The pristine glass bowl was only ornamental now because of Boston's draconian no-smoking laws. Yet Silvia remained a chain smoker outside her office building. "So will you ever forgive me?" she asked.

Fulghum's sharp eyes glanced over the piles of reference works that lined Silvia's back wall, floor, desk and oak library tables. The main part of her desk was occupied by computer paraphernalia and displays. The Boston Globe Archives was one of the world's great on-line news repositories. Still, he saw that on all of the archivist's walls the same original prints hung as before. There were a few personal touches including her diploma from Wellesley alongside her first and second Pulitzers. Silvia was the only person Fulghum knew who kept her office as cluttered as his was though hers was at least spotlessly clean. She also kept a beaver's skull as a memento mori on the corner of her desk.

"Beaver!" he remarked sarcastically. He hoped to break the ice that had formed between them before he took the conversation in the direction he wanted.

"That one's a lot like you, always having to gnaw on something to keep his teeth from growing too long for his own good." Silvia squinted at Fulghum. She furrowed her flawless brow. "You could have called me about Figlear, but you didn't."

He walked over to the library table that held the old-fashioned globe of the world. He turned it on its axis to find Massachusetts. Boston was labeled, but not Pittsfield. "Actually, I like Darcy. She had me stumped with her disguise at first, but the way she held her firearm was pure Agency."

"I hope she survived whatever you two got into. I like her too. She reminds me of the daughter I wish I'd had—or may yet have if I'm lucky." She folded her hands on the table and looked at Fulghum, her eyes imploring him to cut her some slack.

Darcy Figlear had come to John Fulghum's office in the middle of a difficult case involving a female lone-wolf assassin and an Agency hit team. Together they had managed to interdict the four-man hit team sent to murder the assassin on Margareta Island off the coast of Venezuela. In actuality a clandestine CIA operative, Figlear had claimed on entry that she was Silvia's new protégé newshound at the Globe following up on a story that had been spiked. She was so talented playing her role—as well as intelligent and good looking—that Fulghum did not telephone Silvia to verify the girl's story.

He said, "I know why you didn't call me. I suspect both of your phones were monitored from the time the Agency approached you about Figlear. I blame myself for not penetrating her facade. Her disguise was perfect, down to her carrying the Tennessee Squire ID. You briefed her well. She fooled me. To answer your original question, she survived our mission abroad and returned safely to the USA. Where she is now and what she's doing are anyone's guess."

He advanced to run his hand over the top of the beaver's skull. He lifted the skull gently and took the top of the skull in one hand and the jaw on which it sat in the other. He gently put the pieces together again, with the molars occluded and the incisors poised for gnawing. Moving precisely, he put the skull on her desk where it had been and looked Silvia directly in the eyes.

"This is a warning. Turnabout is fair play." He gave her his sardonic smile. Then he slumped into the captain's chair across the desk from hers. The two watched each other for a long moment until Silvia shook her head and looked away.

He noticed her hair was loose around her beautiful face. She was self-conscious about his admiration and used her fingers to pull her hair behind her ears. He knew that in another mood, she might have pulled one strand across her nose like a mustache. She suddenly folded her hands on her desk and in a husky voice asked, "What brings you to my lair this Monday morning, John?"

He thought of a dozen wisecracks but simply said, "Anderson, Stephen. Federal Judge. Boston blue blood. Centenarian. Recently deceased."

He stopped as he saw her hand reflexively reach towards the ashtray again.

"That ashtray is certainly tempting me too. Of course, if you care to step outside into my mobile office, we could both have a smoke while you give me the skinny. Oops. That's not very politically correct of me."

Silvia laughed out loud, slapping the desk to break the tense mood. Fulghum liked that, pointed a finger at her and smiled. She stood, lifted her cardigan off the back of her chair and pulled it on. She absent-mindedly looked in her right desk drawer, then the center drawer, but did not find what she was looking for.

"Damn!" she exclaimed with a frown.

"I've got plenty of Marlboros for both of us." He smiled and gestured for her to precede him out the door.

She raised one finger signaling she had to cover her exit. She picked up her office phone and made a quick call to the City Desk.

"Hi Tony, this is Silvia. I'm going out on a story. Back in the office in an hour. I'll be available on my cell during the interval. Ciao."

She left with Fulghum trailing behind her through the office maze to the street.

When they were in his powder-blue Saab and moving towards the highway, they both lit up and smoked in silence. Fulghum knew she was collecting her thoughts about Anderson.

Silvia's memory was legendary. She was a walking catalog of everything that had appeared in the Globe but also of everything that had not been printed but lay somewhere in the dusty print archives. She blinked in the gray light and squinted before she took a long drag on her Marlboro. She breathed out slowly before she began to talk.

"Anderson, Stephen. Yes, well, his family on both sides was always extremely wealthy and connected almost everywhere to money and power, especially the latter. Married three times. Lucky thirteen children total. Grandchildren in the dozens along with great grandchildren in the hundreds. God knows how many in the next generation after that, but you can bet great great grandchildren aplenty. Always something of a recluse. Korean War hero and received the Congressional Medal of Honor. Retinue of well-paid servants, some foreign, mostly Korean. I met him once twenty-four years ago at a lawn party at his estate on Onota Lake in Pittsfield. Brittle man, handsome and tall, painfully polite and artfully attentive; his Korean companion at his side. Always plagued by relatives wanting his money or influence. His ice-blue eyes sparkled but never settled on anything. He focused on my eyes just once, and a chill ran down my spine. I've never seen such invasive, penetrating eyes. It seemed as if he was looking into my soul."

She paused and thought about what she had just said. Fulghum saw that she trembled slightly at the memory of the old man's eyes. He handed her another cigarette. She took it and smiled, aware that he had broken her trance. He struck a match and held it so she could light up. Then she regained her serious look.

"I heard a rumor he was murdered," Fulghum said to refocus her.

"Forensic work hasn't been completed. Rumors are flying. I believe the Globe reported—and I quote, 'Foul play has not been ruled out definitively.'"

Fulghum thought about that. "The byline for the morning story was Derek Frost."

"Society columnist. Feature writer. He called me for background on Anderson before completing his story. That's why I seem so up to date."

"What's the scuttlebutt inside the paper about the scope and tone of coverage?"

"We've been asked not to sensationalize the Judge's death. Anderson's obit will appear as soon as we've cleared it with the executor, named Dr. Harold Anderson, nickname Harry. There'll be coverage of the funeral, perhaps. Unless something unusual breaks, the story is dead-ended as far as Editorial is concerned. Is your friend Pounce involved?"

Nigel Pounce was the head of homicide for the Boston Police. Complex cases were normally given to him exclusively if a Boston figure was the victim. He and Fulghum had been friends since Fulghum helped with a celebrity murder that occurred in broad daylight right on Boston Common. Fulghum cracked the case when the police were stymied. Since then the detective and the homicide policeman had frequent contact. Fulghum was the unofficial uncle for Pounce's son Joseph and daughter Colleen. Pounce's wife Molly called Fulghum when her husband needed the kind of competent counsel he could trust to be quiet.

Fulghum answered, "I've no idea about Pounce's involvement. I don't even know if the Judge's death's been declared a homicide."

"So you're investigating on a hunch? Is someone paying you to look into the matter? Or did you just want to drop by to pick my brain and admire my legs?"

"Your legs are always worth my time. They always were." He smiled and continued looking out the windshield at the traffic. "Seriously, though, this morning when I grabbed my coffee at Dunkin' Donuts, my young friend Bennie Santorin asked me about Anderson's murder. Without thinking, I quoted a line from an A. E. Housman poem about Mithridates. I don't know why the quote popped into my head."

"Connections that aren't conscious work in strange ways." Silvia mused on this idea. "Terence, this is stupid stuff was the poem. Mithridates is buried in the closing line, or rather not, because he miraculously lived through innumerable attempts at poisoning." She concentrated on the obvious detail. "So poison? By someone who used the same poison on himself as an antidote?"

"I've no conscious idea about that. Why would someone want to use poison to kill someone whose life had already run its course?"

"Where there's a will, there are relatives," Silvia answered with a grim smile. Fulghum knew she was thinking of the infighting among her siblings that had followed her parents' simultaneous death in an automobile accident five years ago. Their wills were bitterly contested by her brothers and sisters and had only recently made it through probate.

"Can you tell me anything about the Anderson family dynamics?"

Silvia drew another deep draft on her cigarette and exhaled the smoke. She lowered her window another inch to let some of the smoke out of the car.

"It's not news that the Anderson family is dysfunctional." She gave her ironical smile.

"In my experience, that's a redundant expression anyway. All families are dysfunctional. Maybe that's the way they ought to define family in the dictionary."

Silvia laughed and nodded in agreement. "Anderson's heirs have been waiting for years for his death, many spending money they don't have with great expectations. Consider that all his children are octogenarians and his grandchildren are sexagenarians. Oops, there I'm being non-PC!" She hesitated for a moment. "Depending on the terms of the will—if one exists, the settlement of the estate should make some heirs immensely wealthy. That's always a motive for murder, isn't it?"

"Put me in the picture with the relatives as much as you can. I'll just listen and smoke while you talk. Here are a couple of cigarettes for you to enjoy in the process."

While they smoked, Silvia gave Fulghum a character-by-character analysis of the Anderson family to the grandchild level. He asked no questions but remembered everything she told him. He dropped off Silvia at the Globe building and watched her all the way to the door. Actually, he watched her skirt swinging against her shapely legs all the way to the door. She turned before she entered the building and with a smile to kill for, waved goodbye. With a mock salute and returning her smile, he drove to his office thinking about the woman's prodigious memory and her alluring legs.

When he climbed out of his car across from Joe's Malt Shop, Fulghum picked up the newspaper and racing form from his back seat. He went through the side entrance that led up a rickety stairwell to the second level above the malt shop. There was his office, littered with stacks of racing forms and illuminated by a small, begrimed window high above the rear of his desk. A captain's chair stood on either side of the desk. An overflowing ashtray was at its center like a used funeral pyre.

Fulghum placed the paper and racing form on his desk and straightened the stacks of old racing forms on the floor. Having dumped the contents of his ashtray into the metal trash basket he kept under his desk, he used his handkerchief to dust off his desktop, chair, and phone. He looked around and dusted his glass display of medals, including three Bronze Stars. The detective closed his office door, sat at his desk and lighted a Marlboro. He then picked up a pencil and, hunched over the Globe, scrutinized Frost's story about Anderson's demise.

It was refreshing to see Silvia again, he thought. She's as beautiful and brainy as ever. We think so much alike, it's scary. It was still a dirty trick for her to send Darcy Figlear into the lion's den with me. Come to think of it, I haven't heard from Miss Agency lately or the assassin whose shapely ass we saved. Maybe it's time for a quarterly postcard, if only I had a current address for either of them. It's time to get down to business. The racing form is calling.

John Fulghum, unlike most other private investigators, had plenty of money. He did not have to take business that ordinary gumshoes could handle. In fact, if a man wanted a stakeout on his cheating wife or a tail on a business rival, Fulghum knew to refer him to Sam Surlick or James Dempsey. If a favorite pet was missing, Fulghum referred the anxious owner to Mark Selvage or Harry Sugden. If a missing person needed finding, Martha Delaney was the person who got the call. Fulghum did not want to waste his time on comparatively minor concerns like those.

Instead, this detective concentrated on cases that somehow did not fit the standard molds. The police had a jurisdiction; therefore, Fulghum might work on a police case that eluded easy compartmentalization. The intelligence agencies also had confining rules that impinged on their operations. The FBI handled cases within the USA, mostly. The CIA handled cases outside the USA, as a rule. Fulghum could work government cases whose boundaries were fuzzy.

As for military intelligence, Fulghum was an expert with extensive overseas experience in war zones. He could accept cases where the uniformed services' investigations were stuck. He could also work where the evidence led overseas for any reason. For murders of his comrades in arms, he knew no boundaries. Solving one such out-of-box case, a veteran found dead in a dumpster, had netted him a large fortune in overseas accounts. Then again, if a case involved horses, he was fully ready to commit his full effort, pro bono if necessary. He had solved the horse lady murders, for example. He had also found a stolen horse the hard way and earned its owner's eternal gratitude.

Absent a current case, Fulghum loved to play the ponies. One of his clients was a gypsy fortuneteller. Her tips had once made him a small fortune. Through her and her husband, he had become a blood brother of a gypsy family with a long suit in clandestine service for the United States government.

Fulghum's list of associates was growing, but he did not advertise his handful of secret friends. Kenneth Mander, the CIA agent, was an example. The PI had worked quietly with Mander on many cases that were too hot for either the local police or the Agency to handle on their own. Fulghum did not make friends easily, but when he did, his was a friendship for life. That went for Silvia, the Globe's archivist, as well as the undercover agent Alia, whom he knew overseas while he was in uniform as well as locally when she passed through Boston tracking tangos. It also went for Darcy Figlear, though they had parted abruptly and might never see each other again. Like him, they were all natural loners and misfits who had an uncommon regard for doing impossible missions for the common good.

Fulghum had no Dr. Watson as his foil and alter ego. He was no Sherlock Homes. The man loved women though he was no womanizer. Strong, brainy women loved him because he was virile, witty and solid all at the same time. The way women could see things as a whole appealed to him. Their clairvoyance complemented his knack for uncannily reliable hunches and intuition.

Fulghum had just lighted another Marlboro. He was about to put his feet up on his desk when his office phone rang to interrupt his reverie.

"This is Fulghum. It's your nickel," he answered.

"Mr. John Fulghum, I don't have an appointment, but I'd like to stop by to talk. I'm willing to make it worth your time." Her voice was husky like that of a mature woman.

"I'm just finishing an important meeting. I have another meeting soon. When would you like to drop by?"

"What if I come in fifteen minutes? What I have to say won't take more than half an hour."

"That'll be fine. Let me check my calendar. Yes, come on by. Do you have directions?"

"Above Joe's Malt Shop, top of the stairwell to the left beside the malt shop's entry."

"That's right. Whom should I expect?"

She had already hung up. Fulghum sighed and went around his office dusting up again. He even dusted his trophies on the table against the back wall. He adjusted the position of his customers' captain's chair. Dumping his new cigarette butts and ashes in his trash can with the old ones, he laid out an unopened box of Marlboros and a book of Boston Hilton Hotel matches. The day's racing form went into the smallest pile of forms against his left wall by the trophy table.

He muttered to himself, "If I were going to do more, I'd have to renovate." With that, he sat behind his desk doodling on a yellow pad with his pencil. Following a random train of thought, he turned the pad sideways and wrote the name Anderson at the top of the page with the names of his thirteen children on the next line, equally spaced. He was about to write the names of the grandchildren on a line below that when he heard a knock on his door.

"Enter. Just turn the knob and push." He spoke loudly enough so that he could be heard through the door. He watched as the shadow of a woman became the real thing as a beautiful twenty-something Korean looking woman dressed all in mourning black entered, adjusting her eyes to the dim light and the ambient cigarette smoke.

"Mr. John Fulghum? The private investigator?" she inquired.

"Yes. Come all the way in and close the door. Please take a seat."

The woman stepped up to the desk in a stately fashion, fumbled in her purse and pulled out a business card. Bowing slightly, she handed Fulghum her calling card with both hands in the Asian fashion, recto up with the text facing Fulghum. Fulghum fumbled in his shirt pocket to find one of his own business cards. He extended his arms holding his card face-up with both hands and bowed slightly while they exchanged cards.

While she made a point of examining his card, he examined hers carefully. Hers, an expensive and tasteful letterpress card with indentation, read, "Kim Su Baek, Executive Assistant, Stephen A. Anderson, J.D., Pittsfield, Massachusetts, USA." No street mailing address or phone number appeared on the card.

"Please accept my condolences, Miss Kim, for the demise of your employer, Judge Anderson. Will you please sit down?"

She sat and took a handkerchief from her purse. She sobbed and dabbed her eyes before she spoke. "Kamsahamnida. Thank you, Mr. Fulghum. It's all so sudden. No one knows what to do."

"I can go down to the malt shop and get you something cold to drink if you like."

"I've been told you have something to drink right here. May I have some of your JD?"

Fulghum nodded. He reached into the second drawer on the right of his desk and brought out two tumblers along with an unopened bottle of Jack Daniels whiskey. He opened the bottle and poured two fingers of the brown elixir in each glass. He handed one glass to his guest.

She lifted the glass and examined the brown liquid. Then she raised the glass.

"Gunbae," she toasted.

"Gunbae," Fulghum said then added,

"'Here's to dear old Boston,
The home of the bean and the cod,
Where Lowells speak only to Cabots,
And Cabots speak only to God.'"

She smiled faintly at his reference to the cream of Boston blue-blood society. They both drank their glasses dry. Fulghum poured more whiskey into both glasses.

"When you say, 'Dry the glass,' you mean it literally."

"You know the Korean language, Mr. Fulghum?"

"Not well, Miss Kim. I studied the language in off moments while I was in the military. I'm a long time student of Tae Kwon Do. I do like Korean poetry, especially by the poet Kim Sowol. What does being an executive assistant to an Anderson mean to you?"

"I know and admire Kim Sowol's poetry. Azaleas is wonderful, but so few poems are in the collection. He died so young. You are a remarkably cultured man. I'm a black belt in Tae Kwon Do. I knew you must have studied the Korean national martial art because of the trophy sitting on the table near the back wall. To answer your question, Mr. Fulghum, until yesterday executive assistant for me meant a good living under difficult circumstances. Today it means I'm jobless but still caught in the middle of family politics and personal accusations of the most demeaning kind."

"The Andersons are right at the top of the social register along with the Lowells and Cabots. Like martial arts competitors, I'm sure they're civil even when under stress."

"On the surface, yes. Underneath, they're like sharks always ready to feed on the weak, starting with the in-laws and continuing to spiral outward with everyone else. Life for them is like a battlefield on which only the fittest survive. Koreans like me are considered to be mere servants."

"I'm sure you're not here to bore me with Anderson family gossip. Why have you come to me this Monday morning? To have three or four fingers of JD? To have me recommend you as a Tennessee Squire? Or something else?"

"Kamsahamnida for the whiskey. I have a very serious matter to discuss with you. I'm willing to pay two hundred dollars cash for fifteen minutes of your time to explore a business proposition." She looked at her Apple watch. "We have ten of those minutes left." She laid two hundred-dollar bills on the desk and looked up at him expectantly.

"Like I said when you called, it's your nickel—well, your two hundred dollars."

"Pardon me?"

"Miss Kim, what have you come to tell me?"

"I've come to tell you that my employer—my father—was murdered."

"That's nowhere in the open news. If you know it's true, why don't you tell it to the police?"

"I can't do that. If I do, the police will immediately assume that I'm the murderer. It will be an easy thing for the family to claim that I extorted the will out of my father and killed him to claim the inheritance. All the relatives hate me."

"As a licensed private investigator, I'm obliged to tell you to report the matter to the police. I've done that." Fulghum was about to stand up and usher the woman to the door. She stood up first quickly and seemed prepared to stop him in his tracks.

"Mr. Fulghum, as you may guess, my life is now in danger."

Fulghum settled back into his chair. "Go on, please."

She sat back down and composed herself, folding her hands in her lap. She spoke reasonably in measured tones.

"Many members of the Anderson family want me dead. If the slightest hint of murder was voiced by me, I'd be targeted and killed. Consider that a fortune close to nine hundred million dollars is at stake. What if all those scores of family members learned that the person to whom the entire family fortune was left by his will was me?"

"Left to you? Can you prove that?"

"I have an original, signed and witnessed copy of my father's will with me now. I'll let you see it if you promise to give it right back to me."

Fulghum nodded. She reached into her purse, pulled out a thick brown envelope and passed it over the desk. Fulghum opened the envelope, extracted the will and read it rapidly. He saw the signature of the Judge and two witnesses at the bottom. The date on the document was exactly one year prior to the present day. He folded the document, placed it in the envelope again and handed it back to her.

"The will looks genuine. Probate will settle the matter. If it's genuine, it can only be trumped by a superseding document with a later date."

"I'm very well aware of that. I have definitive proof that there has been no superseding document." She looked convinced about the truth of her statement.

"And what's your proof?"

"I worked daily with Mr. Anderson through the last trying year. His mind deteriorated in that time, by Alzheimer's, but he was often surprisingly lucid. But the week before he passed, he became rambling and incoherent. I know his lawyer, who also has a signed copy of this will. William B. James, Esq., he's the man who advised me to come to you. He warned me that the Anderson family would do everything possible to have this will destroyed or disavowed or to have me destroyed."

"Do you have the telephone number for this lawyer handy?"

She handed Fulghum the lawyer's business card. The name William B. James conformed to what was written in the will. The detective called the number on the card immediately. A secretary for the law firm Huddles and James answered and routed his call to the lawyer, who verified that what the woman had said was true. He also verified that he was the one who gave the girl instructions to see him. Fulghum hung up the phone and looked at his guest with new interest.

She nodded and said, "Well, Mr. Fulghum, my time is almost up. In my one final minute, will you please tell me whether you'll help me, or not? Mind you, if you say no, I'll have run out of options." She sniffed and dabbed her eyes with her kerchief.

"I need to know more before I agree to make you my client. First, I need to know whether you killed Judge Stephen Anderson." He sat up in his chair and looked her in the eyes. She did not flinch. Her face became serious but not defensive.

"No, Mr. Fulghum, I didn't kill Mr. Anderson." She said this confidently in a steady, firm voice. He was inclined to believe her.

"Do you have an alibi?" The detective opened his eyes wide to give her the impression he was hoping she could provide a credible story.

"I was sent away by his eldest son for the twenty-four hours before he was found dead to attend to a very personal matter. He can verify this. Besides, I'm the Judge's daughter. I couldn't kill my father."

Fulghum looked down at the yellow pad with the names of Anderson's children. With his right hand, he ran her business card under each name on the top yellow page. Her name was not on the list.

"I'm confused. Your name is not listed among the known legitimate children."

"It's correct that I'm not among his thirteen avowed children, but I assure you I'm his daughter and, in fact, legitimate. My mother, who worked for my father for twenty years before I was born, was his concubine. They married in a most private ceremony just after the death of my father's third wife. My mother told me I was conceived on their wedding night or very shortly thereafter. My birth date confirms her allegation. The lawyer and I both have copies of the record of that marriage also."

"I have one final question before I take your case. Do you have any idea who killed your father?"

"That, Mr. Fulghum, is why I'm hiring you. I want you to discover who killed my father and bring him or her to justice. I'm ready to pay you double your usual rate plus expenses with a one-million-dollar bonus for identifying the murderer and another one-million-dollar bonus for bringing the murderer to justice. I've arranged for three accounts to be opened overseas. The money's available right now. I'll turn over to you immediately the operational account with the proviso that you'll return to me any money that you haven't itemized as bona fide expenses. I'll guarantee that I'll give you access to the other two accounts if you deserve the bonuses. If you like, I'll have the lawyer put the terms in writing."

"Please do that. In the meantime, I'll accept your two hundred dollars as my retainer."

Fulghum picked up the two hundreds and placed them in the top front drawer of his desk. By doing that, he had accepted her as his client. She knew it and breathed a sigh of relief. She adjusted her posture and spoke confidently as his client.

"Good. Here's the number of the account at the Scotiabank in the British Virgin Islands and the access code for extracting money."

She handed him two business cards for the bank. He saw that the number of the account was written on the reverse of one card and the account's access code was written on the reverse of the other.

"One thing more - if I should die before you complete your assignment, you are tasked to discover who murdered me and bring the murderer to justice. I've instructed the lawyer to whom you just spoke on the phone to give you access to the bonus accounts in the event of my death. Use the same code to access those two accounts once you have the account numbers. I think that covers everything and I should go." She rose from her chair and extended her right hand across the desk. Fulghum did not shake her hand. His mind was whirling with conflicting ideas about what needed to happen next. His client's safety was the first thing that came to mind.

"Wait a minute. Why don't I arrange for a bodyguard for you? Given the stakes for both of us, I think that would be a good idea. I also recommend placing the Judge's last will and testament in a safe deposit box at a major bank until the dust settles."

She lowered her hand and sat down in the chair again. She appraised Fulghum for a full minute. She became very serious and made him a proposal.

"Mr. Fulghum, if you believe what you say, you'll agree to keep me close to you by making me your executive assistant. You'll then drive me to New York City right now to place the will in a safe deposit box in a bank I know there, the First Bank of Manhattan. I hope you'll pardon me saying that I'm dying for a smoke. May I have one of your Marlboros?"

She crossed and re-crossed her legs provocatively. Fulghum handed her the pristine box of cigarettes and helped her light her Marlboro. He lit one for himself. They smoked while they talked through her proposal.

What the lady said made sense to Fulghum. He would, in effect, be her bodyguard while she posed as his executive assistant. He would guarantee that she remained alive while she transported the will to her bank in New York City. While they were together, she would explain what she knew about the Anderson family and clue him in to her background with Anderson. Fulghum was pleased that his client liked Tae Kwon Do, Marlboros, and Jack Daniels whiskey. That gave them a few things in common besides their business agreement.

Chapter 2

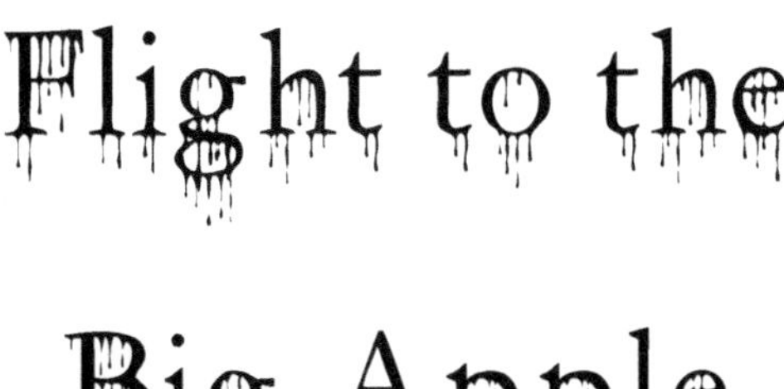

"An American army sergeant [deserter Charles Jenkins] who spent 40 years in North Korea has revealed that the Stalinist state operated a programme to breed spies who could pass themselves off as Westerners." — http://www.telegraph.co.uk/news/ worldnews/asia/northkorea/1471034/North-Korea-bred-spies-using-former-US-soldiers.html

Before they left for New York City, Fulghum packed two bottles of JD in his traveling satchel. At street level, Miss Kim asked him to transfer her large suitcase from her automobile to the back of his. The sky remained gray but not threatening. Fulghum topped off his gasoline and drove the whole way to the Big Apple. Miss Kim fell asleep, awakening only at the tollbooths and their final destination. For the detective the drive was pleasant. He chain-smoked while he kept a close eye out for pursuing vehicles. After the first hundred miles, he was convinced they were not being followed and breathed a sigh of relief.

Fulghum and his client arrived in the city at nightfall and booked two adjacent rooms in the Hilton Times Square. After they were settled, she knocked on his door and suggested dinner. They had an excellent meal with wine at the Restaurant Above. This gave Fulghum the opportunity to find out about his client. After some small talk, with his gentle guidance, she talked about herself.

"Mr. Fulghum, I'm twenty-three years old. As I told you, my birth was a well-kept secret because, even though they were married, it would have been a scandal for a Bostonian of the Judge's caliber to marry his Korean assistant. When I was a toddler, my mother sent me to live with her relatives in Seoul until I was fifteen. I returned to study at Radcliffe College where I graduated with highest honors when I was nineteen. I then attended the Wharton School for a year. After that, my mother called me to Pittsfield to help her tend to my aged father."

Fulghum listened intently. "Korean industry and intelligence certainly pay off."

"Yes, we Koreans tend to work harder than others. Thus we get ahead. I even won top scholarships. I was also lucky because my father paid me a generous living expense allowance under the table. I can document this." Her eyes constantly moved while she spoke. Fulghum knew she was intelligent. He tried to discover what other aspects of her background might be germane to his quest.

"You mentioned that the Anderson family was difficult."

"The correct word might be dysfunctional." She smiled when she saw Fulghum's interest pique with raised eyebrows at the term. "Anyway, my father's siblings, children, and grandchildren were always fighting over money. They're self-centered and jealous, but really they're all greedy wastrels and loafers. Only when I had to deal with the great grandchildren did I encounter real problems."

"What kinds of problems?"

"Illicit drugs, police records, drinking, prostitution - that kind of problem." She uttered this with distaste and ate a sprig of astringent parsley as if to purge the thought. "The men were always after me, pinching me on the bottom and asking me to sleep with them. A couple of the women wanted to get me into bed as well. They thought that because I was a foreigner, I was a loose woman with no morals. Actually, I was too busy with my studies to pay them any attention. When I shifted residence from Philadelphia to Pittsfield, though, it was impossible for me to avoid the Andersons. Everyone closely associated with the estate was poison."

"What do you mean by 'poison'?" Fulghum asked as he sipped his vintage Bordeaux wine and took another bite of his rare filet mignon.

"I mean that the whole atmosphere was toxic. No one said what he meant. Everyone was working on many levels all at once and all at cross-purposes to each other. No one could be trusted for the simplest thing."

"Can you be more specific?" The detective investigated the spring arugula medley with his salad fork.

"Well, within the last year, items started disappearing from the estate. First, it was small things like pieces of the family's heirloom heavy silverware. Then articles of valuable antique furniture, like a Louis XV desk, disappeared. One day a particularly appetitive grandchild showed up with a nineteen-foot U-Haul truck and hauled away Renaissance embroidery pieces, Chinese paintings, and Italian bronzes. After such instances the eldest son, who lived on the estate, would fly into a rage. He would fire the current help and hire new caretakers."

"Except for you and your mother. Why were you privileged?"

"Because my father told him we were special. He'd accept care from no one else. Of course, the butler and housemaid were also exempt from the rule. He counted on them too."

"So the eldest son protected you and your mother?" Fulghum asked.

"You could say that, but he did so begrudgingly. He was always sniping at my mother for the smallest infractions. My mother and I had to work hard to make sure everything was just so for my father, who was losing his competency." She paused. Evidently, that was a major milestone in her personal history.

"What did the eldest son say about his father's mental state?"

"Naturally, he wanted to put my father in an extended care facility. He also wanted to have him declared legally incompetent. That would have given him power over father's money."

"How did you avoid either of those things from happening?"

She hesitated while the wait staff came to remove their plates and serve dessert with coffee.

"This raspberry tort looks appetizing with its jaunty sprig of mint. I'll bet the coffee is better than Dunkin' Donuts coffee too." Fulghum dived right in to savor his dessert.

"To answer your questions, my father came to himself whenever he wanted to. He'd be rambling incoherently for days, but when his eldest son went to him to test his competency, he changed."

"Changed how? By the way, this tort is excellent. The coffee is great too. Eat while we talk. I don't want to eat dessert alone." Fulghum signaled for the waiter to keep his coffee cup filled to the brim.

Ignoring Fulghum's comments about dessert, she answered, "He'd sit straight up in his chair, pull on his bifocals and start quizzing his eldest son about investments. He'd talk about how gold prices were rising, or ask difficult questions about copper, soybeans or pork bellies. He'd ask his son's opinion about writing calls against his stock positions. The eldest son, who never bothered to learn how to manage finances, was always baffled by his father's questions. He'd become frustrated and go away until someone reported that his father's mind was failing. Then the same thing would happen all over again." She took a bite of her dessert and closed her eyes to savor it.

"I suppose your father watched the investment channels around the clock?"

"You guessed it. CNBC was always on except when he was watching Bloomberg. He worked with a number of software packages to buy and sell stocks and options. For example, he used Options Express to sell puts. He also had a huge bond portfolio, which he managed all by himself. I think that's what kept his mind alive all those years."

"Alzheimer's was never diagnosed?"

"He wouldn't let a doctor near him. He took no medicines as a matter of pride. He confided to my mother and me that doctors only wanted to bill and kill, in that order. He was a health nut. I prepared him smoothies blended with vitamin supplements. I also prepared the vitamins and minerals he took twice daily with unsweetened coconut milk."

"You said you'd been sent away twenty-four hours before he passed. What were the circumstances of that?"

"My mother had a severe stroke, and she was hospitalized. I had to rush to the hospital to attend to her. The elder brother urged me to be with her. In fact, I was with her right to the end. Hospital records can verify this. When my mother died, I could do nothing more. So I returned to the estate to discover that my father was dead."

"Did you discover his body?"

"No, I didn't. The eldest son discovered it. He said he entered the room in the middle of the morning and found his father seated in his blue La-Z-Boy chair as usual, but he was no longer breathing. The elder brother told me he had immediately dialed 911. The medics came within ten minutes of his call. They rushed my father to the hospital, but he was pronounced dead on arrival."

"What happened next?"

"The eldest son informed me that, under the circumstances, my services were no longer required at the estate. Since my mother had also passed, I was to pack our things and leave. He told me I should tend to my mother's remains and effects. He gave me an envelope with two thousand dollars in fifties. He said he'd deposit my formal severance pay directly into my bank account. He volunteered to give me a good reference if I wanted to seek employment in the home care industry. The bastard watched over me like a vulture until I was out the front door and driving out of the estate. I stopped by the lawyer's office before I left Pittsfield. Then I drove all the way to your office via Route 9, the Mass Pike and the 128." She was now weeping bitterly. She used her napkin to dry her eyes.

Fulghum let her cry. When she recovered, he said, "So you were given the bum's rush, and you went directly to the family lawyer after that."

"Yes, and I came to you because he recommended that I do that. He said the Judge had explicitly instructed him to send me to you."

"How do you figure that your father was murdered? Couldn't he have just expired as his eldest son said he did?"

"The answer to that question will take time. Let's have a nightcap and retire to our rooms for a visit with Jack Daniels."

Fulghum ordered two glasses of Oban scotch whiskey, neat. Having finished their drinks, he and Miss Kim went down to their floor.

"My room, or yours, Mr. Fulghum?" she asked suggestively as she moved closer and looked up at him with her wide, sparkling brown eyes, so innocent seeming and fresh that a man could drown in them.

"How long will your explanation last, Miss Kim?" He asked to restore the conversation to a professional tone.

"Please call me Sue, Mr. Fulghum." Her hand held his shirt now. Her voice was petulant.

"If you'll call me John, I'll call you Sue. You're paying, so you make the call about the venue for continuing discussions." He said this with all deliberate stiltedness, so she released his shirt and answered him in the same manner and tone as his.

"Very well, John, leave your door shut but unlocked and unlatched so I can get in. Go ahead and pour two glasses of JD with three fingers in each. I'll be right there." She slipped inside her room. Fulghum shrugged and did as his client directed.

He had just finished pouring the whiskey into the glasses when his hotel room door opened. In walked Sue looking like a vision from an oriental painted screen. She was no longer wearing funereal black. Instead, she wore a golden silk robe with red-crowned cranes embroidered tastefully all over it, some in flight and some standing in a meadow of slender green grass. Sue's shiny, coal-black hair was set in the Chinese fashion with two hair sticks holding her curled black tresses in place.

She closed the door and latched it. Then she walked to the table and picked up one glass of whiskey. She wasted no time but signaled him with one curled finger to follow her. She went right back to the master bed, fluffed up two pillows and arranged herself with her legs crossed and her hand patting where Fulghum should recline when he was ready.

"I didn't bring my silk robe or my embroidered pajamas," he confessed glumly. "In fact, I don't own either garment."

"You won't need your robe or pajamas for what I have in mind. I'll try to make you feel less uncomfortable." She rose and dropped her robe to the floor. Her theatrics had the opposite effect of her stated intention. He was decidedly not comfortable until he had taken off all his clothes and the two were under the bedcovers covers naked together.

"Now where were we, Sue?" Fulghum asked.

"The question is, 'Where are we?' Isn't it, John?"

Fulghum knew the lady was correct. He knew just how to console a beautiful adult woman who had lost her mother and father in the last two successive days. He bit her shoulder and kissed her. He used his hands to touch every part of her warm body as she began to weep for joy. Soon she pressed her naked body against him and greedily kissed him on the mouth. He rose above her and looked down into her tearing eyes. With his thumbs, he wiped away her tears. Then he withdrew her hair sticks and set them carefully on the bedside table. She ran her fingers through her hair and spread it on her pillow behind her head. He kissed her gently. She hungrily kissed him back and drew him down into her.

By the time they had finished their explorations and love making, they were both feeling relaxed and ready to drink another glass of JD. She waited until he had fluffed up his pillows and their glasses of whiskey were replenished. Then, like a well-trained entertainer, she began telling her tale, punctuated by his questions as her foot ran up and down his bare, muscular calf.

"I told you my mother gave birth to me while she served the judge. She was called his executive assistant, but she was much more than that."

"How did your father meet your mother?"

"My father was a great war hero during the Korean War. He flew a plane into what is now the Democratic People's Republic of Korea on a suicide mission. The plane was hit by Chinese ground fire and went down in flames, but my father ejected from his aircraft. He was injured when he hit the ground, but he managed to fight his way back south to the American troops. They were surprised to see him because his mission was very secret and dangerous. Everyone thought he would die while executing his assignment. Embarrassed but also pleased by his return, they gave him medals and put him in the hospital to heal his wounds. My great grandmother and grandmother were his nurses there. That was the beginning of the relationship of our families."

"Good Lord, does the connection between him and your family stretch back that far?"

"As far as I know, my father never was intimate with them. He did, however, learn a great deal about my origins from them. You see, my family stems from the ancient royal family of Korea."

"So I'm in the presence of royalty?" Fulghum said half-mockingly.

She frowned and pushed him. "Do you want to hear my story, or not?"

"Continue, Princess. I'm listening."

"In Korea, there's an ancient legend. When the tiger comes down from the mountain, Korea will be healthy. My great grandmother said my father was the tiger that came down from the mountain. He was sent north to die but came back to life in the south. Therefore, he was a godlike man who needed special care for the rest of his existence. She decided our women would care for him until he died. He must have liked the idea because he arranged for my grandmother to come to America with him when he was repatriated. She became his first executive assistant. My mother became the second. For a brief while, I was the third."

"I've read that the Judge had three wives, as well."

"Yes, they came in succession. He married to broaden his wealth and influence. He told me about his wives on one of his lucid days. I could fill you in, but that wouldn't clarify my story or keep it on track." She smiled and took another drink of JD.

Fulghum said, "Okay, we'll skip his blue-blood wives for the moment."

"His what?"

"His blue-blood wives - you heard me correctly. In Boston high society, members of the privileged families marry only others in their same set. If they marry outside their social class, it upsets everyone. Presumably, Anderson's three wives were proper Bostonian ladies."

"All right, I think I understand you. Anyway, my ancestors worked alongside my father even before he was a judge. They became invaluable to him. He believed they had such a strong bond that it could not be broken. So he gave them special missions—things he couldn't ask anyone else to perform."

"Such as? I do like you rubbing your foot up my calf, but I warn you it is leading my thoughts to other things."

She raised her right eyebrow and smiled suggestively. "Hold your thought, John. I have to finish my story."

"What kinds of things did your family do for your father?"

"To give you an idea of what they did, I have to tell you another story. Meanwhile, I'll stop rubbing my foot up your calf. I need you to pay attention to this item too."

Fulghum had risen to the occasion, but now he drank more JD and composed himself. He also reached the bottle on the bedside table and poured them both more whiskey, neat.

"Okay. Tell your tale."

"The royal court of Korea during the Joseon period was full of jealous people willing to do anything to grab and retain power. They killed each other frequently. No one was safe. Because they made rules that killing with knives or swords was forbidden on pain of death, the royal court indulged in poisoning with such subtle concoctions that they couldn't be smelled or tasted, yet they were one hundred percent effective. The best poison was called sayak."

"I've heard of sayak. It's arsenic-based, isn't it?"

"If you've seen the famous film, Arsenic and Old Lace, you know how this poison works. It puts people to sleep quickly and permanently. Anyway, everyone in the royal court of Korea knew about this poison particularly. Women passed the lethal recipe from mother to daughter. I learned about it in the traditional way when I was in Korea at age thirteen from a sister of my great grandmother."

"Wait just a minute here. Is this leading to a confession of murder? I thought you told me you didn't murder your father."

"I didn't murder him. But you need to know the background so you can find out who the murderer really is. Will you allow me to go on?"

"Do me a favor."

"What's that?"

"Don't spike my JD with sayak."

She laughed. "Very funny, don't worry. I need you too much to kill you now. Maybe later." She winked, but he winced. She sighed and frowned at him. Then she smiled and shook her head. Fulghum saw that she could change expression fluidly like the early silent-film actress Lillian Gish. Her expressions portrayed a kaleidoscope of changing moods and poses.

"Now where was I?"

"You said you learned how to make sayak at age thirteen."

"That's right. I also learned later from on-line research that modern forensics can determine accurately whether a person died of arsenic poisoning. This research goes back to the eighteenth century when a case of multiple poisonings in Prussia helped define the signs of arsenic misuse. I've brought my computer. This hotel has wifi. Do you want to read the Wikipedia article on arsenic poisoning?"

Fulghum was curious but still did not want to deflect Sue from telling her story. "Maybe later. Please continue with your story for now. I still don't get the point of it."

"What if I told you my family has been involved in performing political assassinations as long as anyone can remember?"

"You now have my full attention. Please go on while I pour more JD."

"While you're doing that, I'm going to refresh myself in the bathroom."

Fulghum poured the whiskey. He could not help but admire the young woman's physique as she unselfconsciously walked naked to the bathroom. When she emerged, she picked up her refilled glass and touched his glass with it. Then she settled cross-legged with her back straight on her side of the bed to continue her story. He could not tell whether her breasts were real or enhanced. Since they were perfectly formed, he guessed implants.

"I don't know all the details, but I'm certain my grandmother and mother served as my father's assassins, taking care of problem people in his family and businesses."

"Wait a minute. Those are heavy allegations. Do you have any proof?" Fulghum had heard many casual confessions of crimes. This was the first time he heard a young woman nonchalantly implicate her grandmother and mother in the commission of multiple murders.

"Yes. I found a set of black notebooks that document in minute detail the instructions given by my father stretching from the time he was in the hospital in Seoul during the war until my mother took me to live with relatives there shortly after I was born."

"Do you have possession of those notebooks?"

"They're in a safe deposit box at a major old bank in Seoul—Woori Bank in Gwangtonggwan. My mother placed them there. She gave me the key and the code I use to access the contents of the box. Two days before my mother died, she told me where all the successor notebooks were hidden on the estate in Pittsfield. She said if anything happened to my father and her, those notebooks might save my life. Looking back, I find her statement was ominous."

"Where at the estate were you when your mother told you about those notebooks?"

Sue pondered the question. "We were in the kitchen. We were communicating in Korean at the time. In fact, all the records I mentioned are in the Korean language. Some details are also posted in a special code my father invented to hide what he was doing."

"Do you know of anyone else in the Judge's household who knew or knows Korean?"

"My family and the other Korean staff were the only ones who used Korean in my father's household. This allowed us to have private conversations right out in the open."

"Have you seen any of the notebooks?"

"Yes. I flew to Seoul to visit for a week after I graduated from college and before I went to Wharton. I went to the bank; I used the code and key. I saw the notebooks stored there."

"Can you give me the gist of any of the operations described in the notebooks?" Fulghum leaned on his elbow and turned his face close to hers.

"In one case my great grandmother was directed to go to work in the household of a South Korean general who was known to be a traitor. She had to wait until just the right time to poison the man. Subsequently, my father paid her richly for her service."

"I see. Were all the targets described in the notebooks military or intelligence related figures?"

"Actually, no. One target was an American businessman. He ran a large company in Taejon. My great grandmother was directed to infiltrate his household and poison him and his wife. She accomplished her mission. She was paid double what she'd received for killing the treacherous general. She was then tasked to assassinate a person thought to be part of North Korea's spy breeding program. I'm sure you know Pyongyang has had such a program in place for many years to provide North Korean spies with Western characteristics by using American deserters as the fathers."

"Yes, I recall having read something about that program. The original account came from an American deserter who had re-defected. Not everyone here believed his story. Sue, can you give me an example where your father tasked your relatives to use poison against members of his own family?"

"I can give one off the top of my head. My grandmother was assigned to serve as the companion for one of my father's elderly uncles. Once she had gained his trust, she was to poison him by placing sayak in his tea. She was successful and returned to my father's household because her job as a companion was over once the uncle was dead."

"Okay. Let's say the notebooks conclusively show a pattern of assassinations. Let's further say they link your father to every assassination directly. Further still, suppose we can obtain independent verification of the deaths of the victims at the times when your relatives were in their service. What would be gained at this late date bringing this information to light? Certainly, it would do you no good, in fact, it might do you harm by association."

"John, my life may depend on the information in those notebooks. They may also contain the evidence we need to find the real killer." She looked at him over the top of her glass. She sipped her whiskey while he considered her statement. He wrinkled his brow as he was still not convinced of the usefulness of what she had told him.

"Give me an example of a credible scenario by which the notebooks might lead us to the killer."

"What if someone knew exactly what my father was doing? What if that person was waiting for the right moment to take revenge on my father for what he did to a relative or friend?"

'I don't think that's good enough. What does anyone gain from your father's death? Who could have lived as long as or longer than your father to do this deed?"

"I suppose you'd want proof linking the time of the murder to something within the last will and testament?"

"That would be credible. For example, let's suppose you knew your father was going to create a new will that would cut you out of the inheritance entirely. You'd have the perfect motive."

"On the surface, that seems a viable theory. But why would a person murder my mother and father on successive days?"

"You are full of surprises. Do you think your mother was murdered too?"

"I'm convinced of it." Her eyes flashed, and she rose to refill her glass.

Fulghum realized Sue was entirely unaffected by all the alcohol she had drunk. When she held the bottle above his glass, he nodded. She poured him three fingers of the velvety, brown liquor.

"If you're so sure, why didn't you commission me to find her murderer as well as your father's?"

"That's easy. If you find his murderer, you'll find my mother's murderer as well. Because of the timing, the murders must have been committed by the same person. Consider for a moment whether you'd have jumped to help me find the murderer of an elderly Korean woman in the same way you did for what you call a Boston blue blood. Admit it!"

Fulghum saw that the young woman had a fiery spirit. She was spitting out an accusation that made him squirm. Maybe she had a point. Maybe if she had started her initial pitch with the intent to discover her mother's murderer, he'd have sent her to the police or to one of his lowlife gumshoe friends.

"All you say is supposition. We are where we are. You're my client. I work for you. I'm going to find your father's murderer. If I find your mother's murderer, that's all well and good."

Fulghum's cell phone buzzed. He looked at the caller ID. It was Silvia. He answered the call. He put a finger to his lips to indicate Sue should remain silent. She nodded and sipped her whiskey yet appeared to be pouting over the interruption.

"Fulghum here, it's your nickel."

"John, are you okay?"

"I'm fine, Silvia. Why do you ask?"

"You guessed right about the poison."

"What do you mean?"

"Anderson was poisoned. Forensics verified arsenic poisoning. A murder investigation has been opened. Your friend Nigel Pounce has been put in charge."

"Wait a minute. Isn't there a jurisdictional problem with that?"

"The rationale is that the Judge has owned a residence in the heart of Boston for sixty years. So jurisdiction for the investigation has been claimed by the Boston Police Commissioner with the blessing of the Governor of Massachusetts."

"That means this case has the best homicide policeman in the state. I'll bet things are popping as we speak."

"You are right. Pounce has ordered everyone at the estate to stay in place under police guard indefinitely while he accumulates evidence and questions everyone."

Fulghum looked directly at Sue while Silvia said this. He was sure Sue could overhear what Silvia was telling him.

"Hmm. I guessed right. You know how it goes. A kid at the Dunkin' Donuts spreads a rumor of murder. I blurt out a quotation about poison. Et cetera, et cetera. I wish I were as good picking ponies at the track. Thanks for the information."

"Don't mention it. That's all I have, I think. Are you all right?

"Silvia, if you're okay, I'm good for the evening."

"I'm okay, thanks. Oh, one more thing you should know before you go back to your racing forms and your séance with your friend Jack Daniels."

"What's that?"

"The Judge's executive assistant was fired the day he died. The police are looking for her everywhere. Her name is Kim Su something, she's Korean. The police found her car in front of Joe's Malt Shop—in other words, right in front of your office. The girl just vanished into thin air."

"That's troubling. It sounds as if her flight might be a clear admission of guilt."

"The fact she was fired is bothering the police more than the fact that she's flown the coop. The Judge's eldest son is the prime suspect in his father's murder. They're calling it parricide pure and simple. It seems the old man was going to change his will. The police think the eldest son killed the Judge before he could make the change. Are you going to be around tomorrow? I've got a whole boatload of data about your now-favorite dysfunctional Anderson family. Do you want to hear all about it from the horse?"

"Yes, I do. But I won't be around tomorrow. It'll be the day after. Is that okay with you?"

"It's okay by me. By the way, expect a call from Nigel Pounce. He called me to find if I knew where you were."

"What did you say?"

"I told him you're probably where you always are—in your office puffing Marlboros and drinking JD."

"You do know me, lady. Look, thanks for the call. I'll see you the day after tomorrow early if we both can keep alive till then. Have sweet dreams."

"I'd sure like it if you were here with me instead of off somewhere alone. Hint, hint!"

"Me too, Silvia. Bye now." He terminated the call and spent the next minute looking daggers at Sue.

"What?" she asked him.

"You heard what. Let's review the bidding for a moment. Right now you're a fugitive from the law. The estate of your father has been sealed off with no one allowed out or in. It was lucky for you that your father's eldest son fired you and turned you out. Otherwise, you might be occupying a cold cell as he's likely to be doing soon. He's now the prime suspect in your father's murder investigation. The best homicide man on the Boston police force is leading the investigation. Since you're my client, I won't turn you in, but I can't and won't get in the way of an ongoing police investigation."

"So where does this leave us, John?" She ran her foot up and down his calf.

"It leaves us thinking a little faster about a viable scenario. I need to know how we can pull together those notebooks you talked about, if they indeed exist."

"I could fly to Seoul and retrieve the early notebooks from the safe deposit box."

"Do you have a current passport in your possession?"

"As a matter of fact, I do. I'll book a flight to Korea online tonight. After we deposit the will at the bank, you can take me to the airport so I can catch my flight."

"What if the authorities have issued a warrant for your arrest as a suspect?"

"I don't think I have to worry about that."

"Why not?"

She rolled her eyes. Then she straddled him and took his face between her hands. "Because I have a Korean passport. Now that we've solved all the problems that we can tonight, I want to make wild passionate love with you until morning."

"On one condition."

"You've always got conditions!" Sue said petulantly.

Fulghum's face looked dangerously annoyed, like a father about to explode about his daughter's constant complaining.

"Okay, what is your condition this time?"

"Tell me where the notebooks are hidden in Pittsfield."

"I'll whisper their location in your ear." She leaned down to whisper. Her breasts touched his chest lightly, causing him to respond hopefully. The breasts felt real. The detective thought he might have to reassess his initial judgment about them. "They're hidden under the raised marble door sill at the rear entrance. You'll need a crowbar to pry up the marble. The notebooks are packed individually in a sealed box filled with salt to guard against moisture. Now that my mother is dead, I'm the only person alive who can decipher the encoded Korean text."

"I hope we'll find them as you last saw them."

"I satisfied your condition. Now you'll have to satisfy me."

Fulghum did as the lady directed. He worked at it most of the night, but the way she moaned and sighed at first then laughed and cried out in ecstasy at the end, he felt he gave her what she wanted.

He awakened at nine o'clock to the alarm. Sue had departed as her silk robe was no longer on the floor beside the bed. Fulghum rapidly cleaned up, dressed and packed. Then he went to her room and knocked on the door. When she answered, she was dressed in her mourning costume again, only now she was wearing dark glasses. Her face appeared slightly flushed from their nighttime endeavors.

"Good morning, John. I'm packed and ready to go. If you're ready also, we can check out, make our deposit at the bank and get me to the airport for my flight, all by noon. I want to thank you now for everything you've done for me."

She moved close and kissed him sweetly on the mouth - a long, lingering kiss.

Then she stepped back and gestured towards her suitcase. He pulled it behind as they proceeded to the elevator. They checked out, retrieved his car and drove to complete their errand. The bank staff was most accommodating and efficient. He dropped her at the Korean Airways departure area at John F. Kennedy International Airport just in time for her to check her bag and make her flight.

Fulghum then found his way to Interstate 95 and drove straight through to Massachusetts. There he did not visit his office but made a beeline to his apartment. Thoroughly exhausted, he set his alarm and slept dreamlessly until the next morning.

Chapter 3

Onota Lake Estate

"According to the Russian News Agency TASS, 'Arirang is a gymnastics and artistic festival, known as mass games. The extravaganza unfolds an epic story of how the Arirang nation of Korea, a country of morning calm, in the Orient put an end to the history of distress and rose as a dignified nation with the song 'Arirang'. The Arirang performance has been included in the Guinness Book of Records.'" — https://en.wikipedia.org/wiki/Arirang_Festival

Fulghum reached his office five minutes before Silvia arrived with armloads of copies of papers related to the Anderson family. Seated in the captain's chair across the desk from his, she arranged the papers in three neat piles. Satisfied, she looked Fulghum in the eyes and began.

"First, John, your office is a filthy sty. I love you, but you're a slob. Admit it and repent. You should get a cleaning person to give it a once-over every month—whether it needs it or not." She smiled at him brightly. He remained silent, steepling his index fingers and nodding for her to continue.

"Relax, Silvia. Have a Marlboro?"

Across the desk, he handed her a box of Marlboro Reds and a book of matches from the New York Hilton. She drew a cigarette from the box and lit it. She looked at the writing on the matchbook and smiled. Then she passed the box and matchbook back to Fulghum and he lit up as well. They shared his ashtray, which was not the pristine glass of the unused receptacle on Silvia's desk at the Globe, but it would serve. She took a deep draft and expelled the smoke, which mingled with his to spiral up and disappear in the dark recess near the ceiling.

"All right, what I've brought is clearly in three piles." As she recounted what each pile contained, her right hand touched the one she was addressing at the time. Her left hand wielded her cigarette like a baton.

She touched the pile to her left. "This pile is all about our deceased hero. It's everything in the public domain and all spiked stories that never saw the light of day." She paused while he squinted his eyes and nodded. "From this pile, you'll see you're dealing with a national hero of the first rank with an unimpeachable record on the bar and at the bench. What he lacks in philanthropy, he makes up in seclusion and mystery."

She moved her hand to the center pile. "Moving right along, the second pile contains every reference to all of the Anderson clan. Birth notices, marriages, police reports, society articles, everything. I've arranged the articles under fourteen paperclips, one for each child and their resultant progeny. There are fourteen and not thirteen paperclips because the fourteenth clip contains gossip column reports about offspring of mistresses." Again, she paused to gauge his reaction. He remained deadpan and nodded for her to continue. "In this pile, we get the bigger picture of an entire family of wealth and influence marrying into other wealthy families across generations. Clearly, gossip has been managed. Only in the youngest generation has technology made obfuscation difficult. The young lions and lionesses have been busy making fools of themselves in public."

She stopped to chain light a cigarette. Then she laid her right hand on the last pile, a little thinner than the others. "The third pile is my favorite. It contains the hand-written notes of a pair of investigative reporters—let's call them Currier and Ives for fun—who tried to fathom Anderson's war history. Their investigation was summarily terminated by a phone call to the publisher of the Globe from someone way high up in the government. These are copies. The archives hold the originals. They're filed away in the morgue as the Arirang Papers. I can't overstate the sensitivity of these papers. Just what's sensitive and what's not, you'll have to judge for yourself. These records officially don't exist. When you're done with them, please burn them page by page and stir the ashes so no one can reconstruct them."

"Why don't I just bring them back to you?"

"John, I like my job. No one at the Globe knows I made these copies. I'd like to keep it that way. Maybe you'll find something interesting in them. I just don't know. Anyway, this gift more than atones for my peccadillo with Darcy Figlear. That reminds me - Darcy called me this morning just before I left the office to come here."

"Was her call a coincidence? You know I don't believe in coincidences." Fulghum was sitting upright in his chair, his eyes flashing with interest.

"She wanted to know what I was going to tell you about Anderson." Silvia sat back in her chair and took a long drag on her Marlboro. Then she looked at the tip of her cigarette, took another from the box and chain lit it. "She knew you'd be in touch with me."

"What did you tell her?"

"I told her about the first two piles sitting on your desk, but not about the Arirang Papers. I figured she had no need to know about that."

"Did that satisfy her?" Fulghum asked, arching his brow in a way that implied his doubts.

"She wanted me to duplicate everything I was giving to you and give her the second copies. She'll be dropping by my office at two o'clock this afternoon to pick up her set of copies."

"I see. Thanks for the copies and the warning about Figlear. Do you have any other interesting data for me?" Fulghum chain lit another Marlboro and leaned forward to encourage her to talk.

"You'll learn soon enough that the so-called homicide investigation will be limited to forty-eight hours. Frost has been reporting to City Desk from the Judge's estate on Onota Lake. He's also been calling me regularly as well. Not for publication is the fact that Pounce is furious he's only got two days to make his case. He's livid the Chief is trying to rush him to judgment as to the guilt of Harry Anderson, the eldest son of the deceased. Politics and justice—go figure!"

"What's happened so far at the estate?"

"Officers Riley and Shaunessy, working for Pounce, have sealed it off. Pittsfield police are helping to enforce the quarantine. To start things going, Pounce assembled the entire household of twenty-odd employees in the Judge's study yesterday morning. He demanded that none of them leave the grounds of the estate under threat of arrest as an accessory to murder. He ordered an APB for the apprehension of the Judge's Korean executive assistant. She evidently was fired and sent away by the eldest son, Harry, the day the old man died. The Police Commissioner dispatched a police guard and special team, including forensics, from Boston to enforce Pounce's orders while the investigation is in progress."

"I understand what you mean about politics. I suppose Pounce is doing the usual police ritual with regard to a homicide?"

"Pounce ordered a meticulous search of the building and grounds. He wanted a complete inventory of any poisonous substances with their locations. He interviewed each of the household members privately with a stenographer and Officers Riley and Shaunessy present as witnesses."

"All this is standard police procedure. Who are the current suspects?"

"First under suspicion, according to Frost, is Harry Anderson, the eldest son. Second is the judge's butler Albert Maynard. Riley observed that the butler usually is the murderer."

Fulghum laughed out loud and started coughing. He composed himself and told Silvia to continue.

"Pounce is opposed to Riley's view. As it turned out, there was no motive for murder because of the terms of the latest will. Anyway, the butler has an iron-clad alibi - he was absent from the property the previous night as he was at the apartment of the well-known prostitute, Madame Lulu Ko."

"Murder investigations do turn up the oddest associations."

"I agree wholeheartedly. Madame Ko was summoned to corroborate the butler's story. When Sadie Maynard, the butler's wife, heard of her husband's long-term infidelity, she was outraged and flew at her husband with a carving knife but was restrained from castrating him. Having been summoned to appear at the estate, Madame Ko claimed the butler owed her money for her services, but he denied this vehemently. Pounce ordered the prostitute removed bodily from the estate, confident the butler didn't 'do it' this time, if he ever did it in the first place. He returned to sifting his evidence with the help of more sludge and sugar from the nearest Dunkin' Donuts."

They smoked in silence while he pondered her story.

Fulghum was the first to speak. "What progress has the investigative team made with the search for the Korean assistant?"

"I noticed when I arrived here that the woman's automobile is still parked out in front of this building with a ticket on the windshield."

"So that's the car you mentioned when you called me?"

"Yes, it is. I found it odd."

"What?"

"In the morning you spoke of poisoning and Anderson, yet not long afterward, the missing person's car ended up in front of Joe's Malt Shop."

"I find it odd also." He tapped his cigarette ash into the ashtray appearing as if he was lost in thought about the matter.

"I don't believe in coincidences any more than you do, John. Come clean. Was she your client when you came to see me in my office?"

He knit his brow. "Categorically, no!" He stood up, stubbing his cigarette out. "Care to take a drive?" He picked up the sensitive pile of copies and placed them in the right third drawer of his desk, ostentatiously locking it with a small key on his key ring.

Silvia smiled, put out her cigarette and walked down the stairs to his car. Fulghum noticed the plainclothes policeman who was trying to look inconspicuous while keeping his eyes on the vehicle with the ticket on its windshield. Fulghum waved at Joe through the malt shop window. He extended his arm, and Silvia took it. Like a married couple, they walked down the street to his car and settled in for a drive down Route 128.

"Can you tell me anything I don't already know, John?"

"Silvia, I don't know what you know, but I can guess what you're thinking. I do know I'm on dangerous ground. I don't want to involve you. The going may get rough."

She turned towards him, excited by the way things were going. "I knew there was a story in here somewhere. Goody! Can you give me any hints?"

"Ever the newshound, Silvia."

"Ever the gumshoe, John."

"Touche'."

"Well, if things do get rough and you need a place to recover, my door is always open."

"Thank you. I know. The reason I asked us to talk outside my office is that the office may have a new bug. I wouldn't be surprised if this car has a new bug also. I need to get a message to certain people Figlear knows, but I can't be known as the source of information." He paused and looked at her through squinting eyes.

"You look worried, John. It's not like you."

"No, I suppose it's not. Will you give Figlear a message for me?"

"I don't suppose you can write it down?"

"Definitely not. In fact, if you can get Figlear out of your office long enough to tell her the message, it would be prudent."

"I can do that. What's the message?"

"Tell her you need the name and contact number of one of her friends who knows the most about sayak."

"Sayak?"

"Yes."

"Is that the whole message?"

"Yes."

"Should I mention your name in conjunction with this message?"

"No. But when you get the name and phone number from Figlear, call me on my cell phone. I'll see it's you from your Caller ID. I won't answer. Just leave the one-word message 'Mithridates' on my voicemail. I'll drop by your apartment that evening to pick up the information. By then I should know enough to talk intelligibly. I may have entered a killing zone. In that case, I'll not be able to come. If you sense any danger to yourself, call my cell phone and leave the message, 'Dunkin' Donuts.' Then go to the Dunkin' Donuts where we first met. I'll meet you there as soon as I can."

"John, you've gotten me frightened for you—and for me."

"Perhaps it's nothing. It pays to be cautious. I'll drop you by your car."

Fulghum's cell phone rang as he said this. The caller ID was blocked. He ignored the call, which went straight to voicemail. Silvia's phone then rang.

"This is Silvia. Oh, yes. What have you got? No. Have you told City Desk? Busy hell! Look, I'm out of the office, but I'll be driving back there right now. Keep online and talk to me. I'm going to record everything. You've got your other cell phone with you, haven't you? Well, speed-dial City Desk repeatedly until you get through."

Silvia covered her audio input and whispered to Fulghum, "The Judge's lawyer has just been murdered. His office has been plundered and burned. Pounce has ordered the murder scene sealed as an extension to his investigation and not a separate case. It's better if you drive me straight to the Globe. I'll pick up my car later, perhaps this evening. Is that okay with you?"

Fulghum nodded and headed for the Globe. Silvia kept listening to Frost's reportage with her phone on record and speaker. He kept her cigarettes coming, watching for any signs of followers. A maroon Cadillac Coupe Deville seemed to be tailing him four cars back, but he could not be sure. When they arrived at the Globe building, Silvia flung open her door and charged up the steps with her cell phone to her ear. She did not turn to wave before she went through the door.

As Fulghum pulled out, he thought he recognized Darcy Figlear. The lithe woman had Figlear's height and build. The giveaway was her gait. She made a beeline path to the Globe entrance, hell bent on business and so focused she did not notice him watching her. The detective thought of a large clock works with many cogs. It was almost time for Figlear's two o'clock meeting with Silvia. Fulghum edged into traffic and received another call. He recognized the caller ID.

"Hello, Molly! Are you all right?"

"John, I'm so glad to get through. I'm fine, but this has been one nightmarish day."

"Keep calm, Molly, is Nigel okay?"

"Nigel's why I called. He needs your help right away, but he's in a political fix, so he can't contact you directly."

"Can he fish in the evenings out there in Pittsfield?"

"How did you know he was in Pittsfield?"

"I suspect he might want to throw some lines in the water with me at Onota Lake. I can pick him up in my boat around ten o'clock tonight if he's game. I'll bring the bait. Tell him he's to meet me at the pier jutting out from the estate where he's working."

"I'll give him the message right away. Thank you, John."

"Molly, are you really all right? And the kids?"

"We're all fine. I've gotta go now to phone Nigel. I'll talk to you later."

She terminated the call. Fulghum breathed deeply and drew out a Marlboro. He decided he would not return to his office. He found the 128 and headed south to the Mass Pike. It was going to be a long drive out to Pittsfield, but he was sure he could be there on time to make his nighttime fishing date.

From Fulghum's point of view, fishing was one of the best sports invented by humankind. It allowed the mind to follow wherever it was inclined to wander, while beneath the surface, a war was waged for lures, minnows, wet flies or other bait with death in the balance for fish and solutions in the balance for men. Fulghum and Pounce were fishing buddies from way back, for pleasure and business. They fished Pontoosuc and Onota Lakes, particularly whenever they needed to talk. Often Molly Pounce was the go-between when they could not talk with each other to arrange their meetings. Many a tricky case was managed sitting in a small boat with those two men watching a Massachusetts dawn or sunset.

Out on the steel-gray lake in a boat rigged for trolling, Pounce could pour out his frustrations to a like-minded individual who never bullshitted him and never gave him slack. When they communicated, they became one smooth-running machine working for justice in a cruel world of deceit and subterfuge. Molly had done it again, but this time her urgent call was necessary for both men's needs.

Pounce needed to know things a policeman was not privileged to know by the rules. Fulghum needed to tell the police things he could not tell by dialing the usual numbers. It had been a fruitful relationship for over a dozen years. Fulghum had helped Pounce gain promotions and raises. He never asked for money. He never asked for payback of any kind. From the outside, their collaborations would have seemed sinister at best and possibly criminal. Rules were good, weren't they? Of course, they were. The trouble was, the rules allowed hardened criminals to roam free. Expediency sent innocent people to prison for long terms. The bureaucracy often caused easily solvable cases to become cold.

As he drove along the Mass Pike, Fulghum thought about his long history with Pounce, now the head of homicide for the Boston police. They were both Tennessee Squires with tiny patches of land in Tennessee on a plot owned by the Jack Daniels brewery. Joseph Pounce, Nigel's brilliant son, was now an agent of the CIA after proving his worth by solving an impossible case when he was still a minor. Colleen, Pounce's beautiful and talented daughter, had been introduced to the intrepid Deputy Director of the CIA and became her intern and protégé after Fulghum's introduction. If a family existed that was Fulghum's perfect web work of relationships and not at all dysfunctional, it was the Pounces.

Molly Pounce was a Catholic woman who was unimpeachable and unfathomably good. Fulghum, though not a Catholic, thought of Molly as the earthly embodiment of the Blessed Virgin Mary. In this Nigel Pounce, not originally a Catholic but a Presbyterian, fully agreed with his friend and collaborator. Pounce only regretted his busy schedule allowed too little time for him to enjoy the company of his spouse, son, and daughter. So fishing became the way the family, including Fulghum as its extension, came together.

Today the Massachusetts sky was melancholy. The forest-green landscape rose up in splendor to meet the pervading gray. Fulghum thought of the many times he had fished with Pounce. The first time on Pontoosuc, they had both taken record pike and turned them back into the leaden water. "Catch and release" was their policy, and it was wise since they often caught their record fish on subsequent occasions, each growing the legends the two fishermen spun. Joseph was a fisherman too, and during one fishing expedition, he had become a player with his father and Fulghum. The chance encounter changed the boy's life forever and gave the nation another unimpeachable national asset.

Fulghum's friend Kenneth Mander, known as Salamander in the black world that was his métier, was not a lake fisherman. He was a solitary fly fisherman who sought out almost inaccessible streams alone. Nevertheless, he benefitted from the lake fishing that Fulghum and Pounce did together. He tended the boundaries they could not cross. He and his connections patrolled the inchoate territories between police jurisdictions and the broader world where criminals and terrorists held sway. He was a denizen of regions most ordinary CIA agents could not comprehend because of Agency rules and protocols. Why? Because he and the Deputy Director of Operations, a formidable woman named Sheila McCaw, also known as the Crow, could collaborate and range widely in their nation's defense. The DDO became the personal mentor of Colleen Pounce. She also became the personal sponsor of young agent Joseph Pounce. She did these things because of her relationship with Kenneth Mander, who was, in turn, a friend to John Fulghum.

As he drove westward into the sunset, Fulghum thought back through his history with Mander. He had difficulty remembering a time before he numbered Ken Mander among his lifelong friends and associates. Now Mander was his primary Agency contact working at the boundaries of the CIA and local law enforcement. Of course, Boston had its share of international criminal activities. The problem for both the local police and the Agency was sorting out how to handle each case. Sometimes it was necessary for the police to look the other way while the Agency took care of business. Sometimes it was necessary for the Agency to engineer a situation so local law enforcement could bring international criminals to justice under American criminal laws. As a former Special Forces soldier, Fulghum knew the fuzzy boundaries between ordinary law enforcement and the law of the jungle that prevailed outside the continental United States. The detective sincerely hoped his nation would not become numbered among the lawless failed states in which he had labored with the Special Forces.

Before he knew it, Fulghum was turning north towards Pittsfield, aware he was going to be arriving at Onota Lake early enough to rent a boat and fishing gear. He was obligated to pick Pounce up in a boat where the Anderson estate extended down into the lake's water. He found the boathouse and rented the fully gassed-up metal motorboat he wanted for cash with a deposit, promising to return what he had rented before the following dawn. He also rented flotation devices, two cushions, plastic rain gear, two Shakespeare fishing poles fitted with reels and ten-pound test fish line and a large fish net. He bought a can of the bug repellant Off, a pair of pliers and a half-dozen Rapala lures and tied one on each line. He secured the lures by their hooks to the eyes on the rods. Then he stowed the rods in the boat within easy reach and shoved off.

At ten o'clock, Fulghum motored his metal boat towards the pier in the back of the Anderson estate. Not seeing Pounce on the pier, he cut his engine and loitered casting his lure into the night waters toward the shore where light from the estate fell on the glassine surface. Between casts, he stopped to spray his head, neck, arms and ankles with Off. After the sixth or seventh cast of his lure, a bat tried to catch the lure in flight and flew right by his left ear. The light from the pier was cut into silver coins in the black water when his lure hit the surface. He heard crickets and bullfrogs in a rising chorus. At ten thirty, a man walked from the estate proper down to the pier. He flashed a flashlight at the end of the pier, two flashes then a pause before two more flashes. Fulghum responded with the same sequence before he motored to the pier's end and picked up Pounce.

Nigel Pounce climbed into the boat and shook Fulghum's extended hand. The two remained silent as Fulghum shoved off and motored back out into the lake. They were a long way out from shore before Fulghum handed Pounce a fishing pole. Pounce needed no instruction to let his line out behind the boat. In a few minutes, the two fishermen were tending lines running a hundred feet back from either side of the boat. The boat continued running from shore while the men acclimated to their surroundings.

Finally, Pounce whispered, "I'm glad you could come. Things are a mess. The Chief wants me to make a definitive judgment and close my case within thirty-six hours. I needed to talk with you to get options. What do you think?"

"I think your case has become political. Justice will have little to do with the outcome. Though this may be true for every case, the special circumstances of this one will require unique handling."

"How much do you know about this case? I understand a fugitive's car ended up in front of your office."

"As you know, I talked with Molly. I'm glad she and your children are well. I know only a few things about your case. I'm trying to learn more. It's fair to say the Agency is deeply involved. The story goes back at least to the Korean War and maybe to World War II."

Pounce whistled. "What do you think has been going on?"

"I'm guessing at the moment, but the Judge was playing wet black operations. His executive assistants were his arms and legs. Some of his targets were North Koreans actively working against us from within the US."

"Do you have proof?"

"Have your men pry up the marble doorstep at the back entrance of the estate. They must take extreme care not to get anything under the marble moist. You should find records of the Judge's work for an agency of some kind. The records are in the Korean language, and some are in a special code."

"Are you suggesting I should turn the investigation over to the CIA or FBI?"

"You don't know enough to do that now. The Agency will want to put out disinformation about the murder and seek justice on their own terms. Just don't use my name as your source. Say the search was done on a hunch of your own. I think when you find the notebooks, you'll be interdicted right away. I could be wrong. What you find might just be ignored."

"I've just lost the lawyer I was going to use for deep background in cracking my case."

"I know, but his knowledge was limited."

"His office is now a wreck. The bastards who killed him ransacked and torched the place."

"Do you think he had a copy of the deceased's last will and testament?"

"I'd hoped so, yes."

"What if I told you I know who the beneficiary of the last will actually is?"

"I suppose you're going to tell me it was Harry, the eldest son."

"No. Surprisingly, it was the Korean woman tending him during his final convalescence."

"She may be our murder suspect, but no one can locate her. Do you, perchance, know where she's hiding?"

"Nigel, I don't know where she is now. I do know she has access to all the old secret records of the Judge's work."

"And a portion of those records are under the marble on the back stoop?"

"That's so. At least, it's what I've been told."

"Look, John, paint me a picture so I can act within the next few hours and make a difference. If my clock runs out without a solution, I'm finished. Both the Commissioner and the Chief are counting on me. They've made promises to some very powerful people who'll want my head if I fail."

"Relax and tend your line. I'm not sure how much of what I'm going to tell you is true, but if any of it is true, this case is bigger than the untimely death of a centenarian. If it'll help, I brought Jack Daniels to lend a hand through this night." Fulghum handed his friend an unopened bottle of the brown elixir. Pounce opened the bottle and took a long drink. He handed it to Fulghum, who also drank. The detective lit a Marlboro and began to talk while he smoked.

"Nigel, I'm not saying this. You aren't hearing it. I'll deny it if I'm ever asked about one detail I tell you. Agreed?"

"I guess so. Yes. I agree. What've you got?"

"I have learned recently of a history of assassinations stretching back until at least the Korean War, many victims being killed on American shores."

"Good Lord!"

"This is just the tip of the iceberg. Anderson was a war hero, but somehow in the process of his winning the Congressional Medal of Honor, he became involved with the intelligence agencies of both Korea and the USA. He employed workers from the same family who nursed him back to health after his fabled action behind the lines in North Korea. They became his agents and assassins. I don't know who gave the orders, but I suspect they came from the highest levels of both governments concerned."

"So you think the Judge was a clandestine agent of America and a foreign power for over fifty years?"

"I do indeed. In fact, no one but a government could have supported such actions over that long period. A special bond between the control and the agents had to exist during that time so the operations could be continued."

"You're talking murders."

"Yes, and one-half of the documentations of those murders lies buried under that marble slab at the estate."

"You're aware the Judge's lawyer has been killed as well?"

"That makes at least three dead in the last week. The Judge's former executive assistant, Judge Anderson and his lawyer. I expect you discovered all the records at the lawyer's office were destroyed?"

"How did you guess that?"

Fulghum waited a long time before he responded.

"I believe the lawyer was the hidden hand in the operations for at least the last couple of decades. I also believe the assassin who killed him was hoping to eliminate the final will that the Judge wrote as well as the only credible witness to his activities."

"What will was that?"

"It was the will leaving everything to the woman named Kim Su Baek, his last assistant. She's the woman you're trying to find right now."

"Jesus Christ Almighty. How do you know these things?"

"It's better you don't know. It's also better that no one else besides us knows about the terms of the last verifiable will. I believe the inheritance terms will tell us who actually killed Judge Anderson. That's a different line of thought from the long list of assassinations done in the name of national security during the continuing Korean War."

"The man who now looks most likely as the murderer is Harry Anderson."

"I'm convinced that man's innocent."

"Why do you think so?"

"He has too much to lose. Don't forget the Andersons are a venerable Boston family needing the support of the blue-bloods. Harry Anderson is not a Lizzy Borden."

"If he didn't kill his father, who did? My next suspect is the Korean woman who disappeared—the one you say is Anderson's sole heir."

"Nigel, I don't believe she committed the murder either."

"Wow. What makes you sure she didn't?"

"Are you aware she was the deceased's daughter by his fourth wife?"

"What? I've been over this case with a fine tooth comb. Anderson had three wives and by them, thirteen children. Now you're telling me there was a fourth wife and a fourteenth child. You're also telling me she was made his sole heir. That breaks every rule of the social code in New England."

"Nigel, sometimes when you go for the truth, all the old paradigms fall by the wayside. I won't violate client privilege by telling you I have access to the evidence of the Judge's fourth marriage. I also have access to the birth certificate of his daughter."

"This is almost too absurd to be true."

"There's more. I know where the final signed and witnessed last will and testament is right now."

"You do? What are you saying, John?"

"I'm saying the latest assassination of the lawyer was not sufficient to eliminate the will in question. The perpetrators may have thought they destroyed the will, but they didn't. They hoped the fourteenth child would be incarcerated and silenced. Instead, she escaped the state and the country. She's right now obtaining the records you won't find when you look under that marble slab tomorrow morning."

"What records are those?"

"The records that go back to the Korean Armistice. Those will connect the current history to the distant past. Looking at the whole picture will give your investigation the perspective you'll need to discover the true offenders."

Nigel was silent while he pondered what Fulghum had said. He drank Jack Daniels whiskey and passed the bottle back to Fulghum. They tended their lures while the moon continued its nocturnal travel. An otter broke surface near the boat and sank again. Far off, a loon uttered its mournful cry.

"John, I need to talk with your client."

"In due course, you will. Right now, her life's in danger. Consider that she's the only link between the historical data and the Judge. Now that the lawyer is dead, she's all alone. Whoever killed the others will probably try to kill her also."

"How did she come to you?"

"The lawyer sent her to find me after she'd been dismissed from her employment. The Judge had given his lawyer instructions to send the girl to me if anything went wrong. I don't know why he did that. I never knew him."

"Stupid Harry Anderson! If he hadn't sacked the girl, we'd be able to question her right now."

"Often doing the expedient thing is wrong in the long term. In fact, the eldest son's peremptory action may have saved the woman's life."

"I can understand that. I'm not pleased, though, you didn't connect me with her right after she contacted you."

"You'll have to live with that, and so will I, Nigel. I went with my gut instinct. Do you want to know more?"

"I feel supersaturated now, but I'd better hear it all. We may have difficulty communicating again before this case is terminated by higher authority."

The two passed the bottle of Jack Daniels back and forth as the motorboat turned back towards the pier where Fulghum had picked Pounce up. Fulghum spoke in whispers because he knew how far sound carried over still water.

"The EA's family is connected to the royal family in Korea."

"Korea doesn't have a royal family."

"Not today, but Korea was once ruled by kings with big, contentious families. They are masters of poisoning, with a substance called sayak. The art passed from mother to daughter. She learned her skills from her mother and grandmother. I'm convinced they were all agents of the KCIA, the Korean counterpart to our Central Intelligence Agency. Kim Su Baek is a genius and well trained. She's also a Korean citizen and probably KCIA."

"Assuming all this is true, what mitigates their having committed murders on US soil?"

"The Korean War never ended. An armistice has held the conflict in limbo since the actual fighting ceased. It's a Korean Cold War that has outlasted the Cold War between the US and the USSR, though the two are certainly related. During the continuation of the Korean War, agents of the Democratic People's Republic of Korea or DPRK have infiltrated the United States. KCIA agents have infiltrated the DPRK. Enforcement had to be handled by some entity, but it couldn't be handled here by the CIA or FBI."

"Why not?"

"Because neither organization could be trusted at the level we are talking about."

"So what do you think happened?"

"I think the South Koreans created Anderson as the dream connection that would last until he died. They used him by joining him with their trusted KCIA agents, who kept him alive all these years. You have to understand how important lineage is to the Koreans. They had to have a guarantee that their interests would be protected. Anderson was their trusted enforcer in the USA. Whenever the South Koreans discovered a North Korean agent had been infiltrated into America, they sent Anderson the details, and he took care of the problem."

"You mean, he killed on orders."

"I mean exactly that. Our CIA's hands were tied. Our FBI had to look the other way. Our people couldn't be counted on to remember what was at stake. Anderson remembered. He was remarkable. His son was not worthy to succeed him. South Korea must have been desperate to find a replacement in the event of the Judge's death. While they deliberated, they played with fire and prolonged his life."

"He lived over one hundred years. Do you mean to say he remained active until he died?"

"Yes. Every time it was rumored that his wits were failing, he rallied. His mind could run circles around his eldest son's mind."

"So in the end, he had to die."

"Yes, but he was not ready to die when he expired. He was pushed over the line by someone."

"Do you know who that someone was?"

"Not yet, but I'm working on it."

"I can do only two things. First, I can lift the marble slab and find what's under it. Second, I can refocus my search on everyone except the eldest son and the former assistant. In the meantime, if you get the chance, tell Kim Su Baek I'd like to talk with her. I won't violate her security, but I desperately need to connect the dots and find the killer."

The boat was running up to the pier at the Judge's estate. Pounce made up his fishing pole. He shook the detective's hand and prepared to climb out of the boat. Fulghum steered the boat so Pounce could jump onto the pier.

It was a smooth execution. As soon as Pounce had leapt to the pier, Fulghum revved up his motor and drove along the shore to the boathouse. There he made his line to the cleat that belonged to the boat. He dropped the rented gear at the drop off point. He stowed the Off and extra Rapala lures in his trunk.

He climbed into his car for the long drive home to Boston. He was exhausted, but he reminded himself of his work in Central Asia, which never ended. Always on watch while in uniform, he was a numbered national asset. He knew the stakes and what was required of him.

Fulghum checked his cell phone messages to find one. Silvia had left the message, "Mithridates." She had not invoked their emergency protocol yet. He knew he'd have to rush home to Boston, but her life was not in danger.

He responded to her message with a simple "K" and drove into the Massachusetts night.

Chapter 4

The Usual Suspects

"The Korean Armistice Agreement is the armistice which ended the Korean War . . . The armistice was signed on July 27, 1953, and was designed to 'insure a complete cessation of hostilities and of all acts of armed force in Korea until a final peaceful settlement is achieved.' No 'final peaceful settlement' has been achieved yet." — https://en.wikipedia.org/wiki/Korean_Armistice_Agreement

John Fulghum drove straight through to his apartment. He fell asleep immediately and awakened to the sound of his cell phone ringing. He saw the call was from Silvia.

"Good morning, John. It's Silvia. Do you want to hear the latest now or read it in the papers?"

"Hello Silvia, you know what a news grabber I am. What's the scoop?"

"Your friend Pounce had moved right along his list to suspect the estate gardener and his wife because of their use of many poisons while taking care of the venerable house and grounds. The police search of the premises yielded a wide variety of toxins under the immediate, locked care of the gardener and his family. They, therefore, had the means of killing the Judge, but nothing in the deceased's autopsy indicates that any of their cornucopia of poisons was used to commit the murder. The Judge's lawyer attested before he died that, as with the butler, there should have been no great expectations based on the terms of the latest known will."

"So no motive for their having killed the Judge was apparent. Why am I not surprised? I'll bet the pair stood to benefit from the Judge living as long as possible."

"According to Frost, if the lawyer hadn't died suddenly, the complex trust arrangement might have had an interpreter. Pounce ordered copies of all pertinent trust documents to be provided immediately. He also summoned the banker who managed the trust funds. He learned from him that nearly all the funds had been exhausted or pledged against loans."

"So you're telling me Anderson's legacy was a hollow inheritance?"

"Everything was in hock at least once over. If the Judge had an estimated wealth of nine hundred million dollars when he died, after paying off all his estate's debts, he would have been lucky to bequest five million or so after estate taxes. That's the extent of this grand old family's assets."

"If his heirs knew this, they'd not be able to pay off the debts taken on the understanding that when their boat came in, they would be rich as Croesus."

"Does that give you a warm, fuzzy feeling, John?"

"Are you ready for company tonight with a gumshoe Romeo?"

"For Rudy Valentino, no. For you, certainly. In fact, I'll put on something special."

"For dinner?"

"That too. Is seven-thirty okay? I'll be running a little late at the office to tie up some loose ends."

"I'll see you then. If something comes up in the meantime, I'll call you on your cell. Please do the same for me."

"If you're late for my soufflé, I'll eat it all myself and to hell with you."

The detective hesitated while he assessed what she was really saying. "I'll be there, on the dot."

Fulghum was anxious to discover the information about Figlear's Agency sayak connection, but he had been neglectful of Silvia. Tonight was the night when he'd make up for all the lost evenings when one or the other of them had been too tired to contemplate being together properly.

Fulghum actually brought cut flowers to her door. She embraced him and rushed the flowers to her sink where she expertly trimmed them and arranged them in a vase for the table's centerpiece.

"It's been much too long, John."

"I agree. Think of how difficult it would be for us to live together. You're always on call at the Globe. I'm always being pestered by my clients."

As if on cue, Fulghum's phone rang. He saw the caller was not identified. He let his voicemail record a message.

"Something certainly smells good tonight."

"In addition to the soufflé, I made crab cakes with coleslaw especially for you."

"My favorite. How do I rate that?"

"It's like the grace of God, no one deserves it. It just happens. Will you please set the table?"

"Shall I set for two or more?"

"Silly, the plates are in the cabinet. I've chilled some Chablis. Use your flowers as the centerpiece. Light candles if you like. Consider this as a romantic evening. Hurry! The soufflé will be ready in one minute, thirty seconds. The clock is ticking, or it would be if it weren't digital."

"Nothing could be better. You don't know it, but last night I motored around Onota Lake all evening."

"Hmm. Pittsfield. It's a long drive out and back. You must be exhausted."

"I caught a few winks. Have you been busy?" He finished setting the table while he spoke.

"Non-stop. Oh, yes, the Anderson case seems to have a few new wrinkles." She paused to gauge his interest, waiting the final seconds for the soufflé.

"Do you have any Jack Daniels?" he asked.

"As a matter of fact, I just stocked away four pristine bottles of Number 7 for a special guest. Since you're here, we might as well enjoy it. Make mine two inches. You can pour yourself as many as you like. Quick! The soufflé is ready. I'm taking it out of the oven now. Let's sit right down."

They sat down, and she spooned the soufflé onto two plates. While they ate, Fulghum was effusive in his praise of the chef.

"This soufflé is outstanding. One day I'm going to recommend you becoming a Tennessee Squire."

"What do I get for that? Mmm. The soufflé is good, if I do say so myself. I never make it unless I have a guest. I'm glad I'm not out of practice."

"As a Squire, you'll get invitations to special events in Tennessee. Notifications of new liquid concoctions, that kind of thing."

"I like the fact a Squire comes visiting once in a blue moon to have dinner."

"Do you know what a blue moon is, Silvia?"

"It's the second full moon in the space of a month."

"That's correct. Now for double jeopardy, do you know what a gibbous moon is?"

"When I was little, I thought the word was 'gibbon.' I couldn't figure what a monkey had to do with the moon. Gibbous is a moon between half and full. It's a half moon with a bulge, like it's pregnant."

"The lucky lady is a winner. Your message indicated you now have the name and contact data for the sayak person at the CIA."

"Is that my double jeopardy?"

"It depends on whether the data pans out."

"First, tell me what you can about the Anderson case."

"Patience. Our places are set. We've devoured the soufflé and are calmly awaiting the crab cakes. I now need two tumblers and ice for the JD."

She filled the tumblers with ice and gave them to him with a cheek extended for a kiss. With a look of bemusement, Fulghum set the tumblers down and pulled her close for a proper kiss on the lips. Silvia melted in his arms and held his attention for a bit longer.

"Now I feel much better," she said when her head cleared. She turned away so he would not see her tears well up.

"Silvia, what would I do without you?"

"We haven't yet figured out what you're going to do with me." She looked over her shoulder with a suggestive smile as she put the crab cakes in the hot oil.

"I do like your crab cakes."

"I like cooking them for you. Like I said, if I'm only cooking for myself, I get bored. Your contact is Rex Mason. His number is right here in Massachusetts, 978-603-3330. Are all CIA phone numbers divisible by nine? Never mind. Darcy told me I owe her one for the information. She also said to say hello to you. The way she looked at me, she seemed like a co-conspirator. John, you haven't been sleeping with the help, have you?"

"With prim Miss Radcliffe? You must be joking. I like amplitude as well as pulchritude. Something like a romp in the woods?"

"I don't know whether to believe you, but I like the sound of what you're saying. I don't know whether to turn off the burner or wait until after we eat dinner to turn up the heat."

"Let's have things both ways, shall we?" He walked up behind her and wrapped his arms around her. He felt her sigh and press back against him.

"Burning the candle at both ends always gets us into trouble."

"Do you object?"

"As long as the flames continue, I'm satisfied."

"As long as I can satisfy you, I'm happy."

"After dinner, I'm going to hold you to your word. When was the last time we took the time, John?"

"Far too long ago. I'll pour the wine. Those crab cakes look just about done."

They ate her crab cakes with two different sauces, white and red, and drank the Chablis until the bottle was empty. Afterward, they started on JD as Silvia served a raspberry tart she had baked. She put a dollop of fresh whipped cream on each portion.

"The Anderson case is getting more complex by the day." Silvia drank a sip of her whiskey and raised her fork to attack her tart.

Fulghum hesitated with his fork in mid-air. "Why do you say so?"

"The police apprehended the Korean executive assistant when she got off her plane at Logan on her return from Korea. She's been driven to the Anderson estate for questioning. The latest I heard from Frost was that she is now the number one suspect in the murder investigation. She's got a crazy story about her being a legit daughter of the deceased. She says the Judge left his entire fortune to her. More than that, she says she's got proof certain. Imagine!"

"How much longer has Pounce got on the case?"

"That's the funny thing. All the nonsense about having two days to seal things up went out the window when the girl reappeared. Now the brass wants her declared the murderess as soon as possible. Your friend Pounce is likely to get another medal. I'll bet he'll be chief one day if he plays his cards right. John, are you all right?" Fulghum seemed stunned by the news.

"Oh, yes. I'm fine. I was just musing. As soon as you've finished your tart, perhaps you can join me in your bedroom. I think a visit to paradise may be right around the corner."

"Promise?"

"I solemnly swear."

"Hmmm – as it happens I'm finished now."

"Well, then. Sounds like a good time to journey to the bedroom."

He rose and lifted her bodily from her chair. She wrapped her arms around his neck and smiled. After carrying her to the bed, he gradually took off her clothes. Silvia allowed him to take his time and watched him enjoy her curves. Slowly, John disrobed and slid into bed alongside her. She took a moment to breathe deeply and relax as he kissed her gently. Their desire grew passionately when she kissed him back.

Fulghum knew Silvia as he knew no other woman. She understood he would guide her where she needed to go. All night long, sharing their bodies and desires, he set her sights on paradise. When she arrived, he understood he had only a small amount to do with it. She achieved her glory all by herself. When they parted, her hand reached out to stroke his chest. It did not really matter it was John Fulghum's chest she was feeling. He was a man. She had been satisfied. It was enough.

The next morning before Silvia awakened, John had risen, showered and departed. He left a note under the flower arrangement on the table. "A night never to be forgotten! Let's do it again soon. You are one of a kind. Thank you. Love, John."

Fulghum had left early because he needed to call the number Silvia had given him. When he did that, the male party on the other end told him to meet him at the restaurant where Orson Wells had eaten his three dozen oysters, washed down with bourbon. Fulghum had just enough time to navigate the morning traffic and arrive in time to order his first dozen oysters. His contact moved up right beside him and ordered a dozen oysters for himself.

"Rex Mason. You asked to see me?"

"Yes. I need to talk about an ancient Korean tradition that continues today."

"I think I know what you mean. I take it you're not cleared and adjudicated to know such things."

"That may be true, but I have records that might interest you and your people."

"Records, perhaps, of certain wet operations?"

"Yes, in Hangul, encoded. The records go back a half century in an unbroken line."

"I'm sure you know how dangerous it is for you to have those records."

"I do. I want to get rid of them as soon as possible. But I also want to make sure they get into the right hands. I'd be upset if I should discover they were misused. I also want information for conveying those documents."

"We'll be willing to pay you a lot of money instead."

"What do you consider a lot of money?"

"We'll pay one hundred thousand US dollars for each notebook into an offshore account you would control exclusively."

"I don't want your money. I'm trying to save a life. I need information."

"That would be a problem." The young man seemed uneasy now. He was certain the promise of money would get his masters' intended results. Now that Fulghum had refused the offer of money, he was unsure what to do next. He had not received instructions for exchanging information for the documents.

"Let me ask a leading question. May I?" Fulghum asked.

"I guess so."

"Who in your organization is qualified to trade my documents for information?"

"You don't have the clearance or the need to know. I'd say only the Director could authorize the trade."

"So go back to your minders and get word to the Director that I have the documents. If there's no trade, I'll use the documents however I need to get what I want."

"What do you want?"

"I want three things. First, I want Kim Su Baek freed from any retribution or prosecution. Second, I want to know the name and contact information of the current lead for the program to keep an eye on North Korean agents in the United States and interdict their operations. Third, I want a list of all victims terminated by the Korean assassination team that were not national security risks at least back to the end of the Korean War."

"You don't want much, do you?" The young man remarked sarcastically as he ate another of his oysters.

Fulghum got a fixed, serious look. "Look, Rex, or whatever your real name is, my deal is simple. I want all three things, or there is no deal. If you intend to answer by threatening me or intimidating my friends or me, I'll make a big stink. People will get hurt. Do you understand me?"

"I understand you perfectly." The man's hand shook as he raised another morsel on his oyster fork.

"Good. Now let's talk about the unoffending topic of sayak." Fulghum returned to his oysters. He drank bourbon after every bite just as Orson Wells had.

"Sayak was the ritual poison to eliminate members of the Korean royal family in bygone days when Korea was ruled by a king."

"And one poison used until very recently for assassinations by Korean agents against targets here in America."

The young man twisted in his seat but nodded uncomfortably.

"As a good faith measure, I expect your bosses to be in touch with the Chief of Boston Police to arrange the freedom of Kim Su Baek within twenty-four hours. You know my cell phone number. You or your people will call with the simple message that you will give me the guarantees I need. I'll set the terms for the transfer of the documents for the information at that time."

The young man nodded.

Fulghum raised his hand and ordered another dozen oysters on the half shell. His companion decided against having a second dozen oysters. He finished his last oyster and his drink. He dropped a fifty-dollar bill on the table. Then he rose and left the restaurant quickly without shaking Fulghum's hand or looking back. The waiter cleared his place and brought Fulghum a second round of shellfish and more bourbon.

The detective took his time and savored every bite and sip. He wondered how Orson Welles had managed to down not two, but three servings of raw oysters at a sitting. Then he thought of the man's enormous girth. He shuddered when his cell phone rang.

"Fulghum. It's your nickel."

"John, it's me, Sue."

The detective dropped his head and looked around while he switched his phone from one hand to the other. He could not believe the Agency could have moved this fast.

"Sue, how are you? And where are you?"

"I'm fine. I'm just leaving the Pittsfield estate. I've just been informed I won't have to stay here at the estate after all. There'll be no intensive interrogation. I'm free to do as I please. I thought maybe we could meet and talk. I've got lots to tell you and something to give you as well."

"Do you remember the room where we first met?"

"Of course, I do."

"Meet me in the rear of the establishment below that location tomorrow at noon. I don't want to talk more now. Can you meet me there, then?"

"Yes."

"Watch your back. If you encounter any difficulties, call this number. If I don't answer, leave a brief message stating whether you are okay or not, where you are and how long you will be staying there. Will you do that?"

"Yes. I think I'm being followed now."

"You must count on being followed from now on. The question is whether you're being threatened by the people who are following you."

"How will I know I'm being threatened?"

"Probably you'll only know when it's too late to do anything about it."

She laughed uncomfortably. "I'll see you tomorrow."

Fulghum finished his meal, paid the bill and left the restaurant. He drove first to his office to pick up the papers Silvia had brought then he proceeded to his apartment. He laid the papers on his kitchen table and fetched a crookneck lamp by which to read them. For the next five hours, he pored over every document until he had memorized all the salient records.

Fulghum discovered the reporters' notes were a bonanza. He learned through them that the Judge while in uniform had fought his way back to the American lines not alone, but with a prisoner not mentioned in any of the public records. His prisoner was a Soviet advisor to the North Korean regime. The military personnel whom Currier and Ives had interviewed about the true facts about Anderson's escape from the North to the South gave them little information because of classification issues. The spokesmen did not deny certain facts, including the fact that Anderson's target on his airborne mission was to bomb a well-protected biological warfare center. After accomplishing the bombing mission, his plane was shot down. The Korean agents who protected him during his escape provided information about the Russian advisor's critical involvement in the war and his current location. Anderson worked with those agents to apprehend, sedate and convey the Russian officer first to American forces and then to the intelligence chief at the United Nations Forces headquarters.

While Anderson's classified mission earned him the coveted Congressional Medal of Honor, his private initiative to capture the Soviet operative was considered an embarrassment. Anderson threatened to make the true facts known until a trade was arranged, exchanging the Soviet agent for an unspecified number of American POWs held by the DPRK forces and the Chinese Army. Two reporters interviewed Anderson, but it was unacceptable to take any notes. In the Arirang Papers, Fulghum discovered Anderson was furious about the release of the Soviet operative. In this matter, he was in complete agreement with the South Korean agents. That plus his regard for his Korean nurses in the hospital forged a bond between him and South Korea, which endured. Currier and Ives wrote they were convinced Anderson was an active agent of South Korea at the time.

Fulghum shook his head when he read this. Cynically, he wondered how Anderson managed to remain alive after surviving an impossible mission and accomplishing a separate operation that caused a widespread cover-up, which must have gone right to the top. The explanation may have been as simple as the reporters speculated—a proper Bostonian could not be summarily executed for assisting a foreign power allied with the United States. The detective figured the reporters' knowledge alone allowed the Bostonian to live. If Anderson had met with a fatal accident on a subsequent mission, Currier and Ives might have written something about the interview the authorities could not silence. Fulghum scribbled down a couple of names of Koreans the reporters mentioned. They were involved with Anderson while he was in the hospital. Afterward, he concluded he had better destroy the documents immediately.

Fulghum picked up only the documents Silvia wanted burned after reading. It was late, but he immediately drove to a farm in Milford, New Hampshire, where he did his target practice. There with a pen light he found an empty oil barrel in a field and set a fire in the barrel. Page by page he burned the papers he had promised to destroy, taking care not to have the fire spread beyond the barrel.

He did not burn more than one page at a time. Each page burned slowly, the fire eating the paper from the outer edge toward his thumb. The papers glowed in the night like red worms of fire. When he had burned all the pages, Fulghum stirred the ashes with the snapped-off portion of a fallen black branch. Satisfied, he drove back to his apartment. While he drove, he called Silvia's cell phone. She did not answer, so he left her a short message, "Destruction is complete. Fulghum."

The detective was tempted to go to Silvia's apartment door as a surprise. He decided against the idea since he valued privacy as much as she did. As he entered his apartment, he received a call from Kenneth Mander. The CIA agent wanted to meet immediately in his office with Jack Daniels and himself attending. Fulghum had half-expected Mander's call. He did not hesitate except to splash water on his face and dry it off. He made it to his office inside half an hour and found the CIA agent sitting at the top of the stairs outside his office.

"Hi, Ken."

"Hi, John. Sorry for the late meeting. National security never sleeps."

"Fortunately, neither does Jack Daniels."

Within five minutes, the men were seated on opposite sides of Fulghum's desk drinking their first glasses of Jack Daniels whiskey.

"What's on your mind, Ken?"

"Do you mind if I play with one of my toys before I begin?"

"Be my guest."

Ken raised his two fingers to his lips to signal silence. Then he reached into his pocket and pulled out a small electronic device. He walked around the office and behind Fulghum's desk where he was rewarded with a signal from the device. He gestured for Fulghum to open the second drawer on the left side of his desk and felt the underside until he found the bug planted there. After showing him the bug, Ken sealed it in a Ziploc bag and continued scanning the office until he was satisfied no more bugs could be detected with his hand held device.

"You may not be entirely clean of bugs. I got the nastiest of them in any case. You can keep it as a souvenir." He tossed Fulghum the bag with the bug. Fulghum caught it. He opened his floor safe and stuffed the bag inside. He closed the safe and spun the dial. Then he turned his chair towards Ken and opened his hands.

"So talk."

"I understand you met Terry Anheld earlier today. He's one of our young Korea hands. The DDO told me he has a problem with your demands for certain documents you've found."

"He called himself Rex Mason. They seem to be reasonable requests to me."

"To show good faith, the Director made a few calls. Kim Su Baek was freed immediately. We happen to know you were contacted by her shortly after that happened. From what the two of you said, she's got a package for you. I'm here to tell you the package she's carrying is hot. She's in a red sector. Meeting you will put you in the same red sector also. What gives with you two?"

"It's a long story."

"So let's bring JD into the picture with us. I've got all night."

Fulghum told Mander the story of Kim Su Baek and their meeting, omitting only the intimate details of their connection. He explained how he helped her get to New York to place her document in a bank safe deposit box and advised her to fly to

Seoul to fetch the notebooks she claimed were in a bank safe deposit box there.

"I think the package she's bringing me includes the notebooks that were in her safe deposit box. Do you want to see those documents too?"

"I don't really care what's in those documents. I only know from the Crow that they're extremely hot articles. Sue's in deep trouble until she gets rid of those records in a way the opposition will understand she's no longer in possession. Whoever receives them is then in a red sector. Bad fortune will follow the chain of custody. I'm convinced of that."

"Let me guess why. Those notebooks contain evidence of a series of illegal wet black ops both in Korea and on American soil. Am I warm?"

"You're blazing hot. They also describe sources and methods on a joint op between the US and South Korea going back to the end of the hostilities phase of the Korean War. Sources and methods are a hot wire, as you know. Everything and everyone associated with those operations is either cleared TOP SECRET or dead, with no exceptions except for Sue and you."

"This much I surmised. What's the Agency connection to Kim Su Baek?"

"She's a KCIA assassin, trained in her early teens to follow in her grandmother's and mother's footsteps. She's one of the new school of spies. Her forebears played by the old rules and antiquated technologies. She's got a whole new bag of tricks. Do you know what field her Radcliffe degree is in?"

"No. I didn't think to ask her."

"It's a double major in biochemistry and human physiology. She wrote her undergraduate thesis on the synthesis of undetectable toxins. Did you check on what she was doing at Wharton?"

"Again, no."

"She was specializing in the mechanics of start-up biotech companies."

"Any idea what her aim is?"

"No, but one thing's for certain, whatever it is, it's not her aim, but South Korea's, specifically the KCIA's."

"I've been trying to sort out who killed her father in Pittsfield. That's the extent of my interest. The rest came out as I followed the quest to satisfy my client."

"We've also been trying to figure it out. Our real concern is not the perpetrator but the timing of the murder."

"Are you looking at his death in isolation or combined with the death of Sue's mother and the old man's lawyer?"

"We at the Agency try to see things whole, at least the Crow and I do. The best we can come up with as a working hypothesis is this - the old man was showing signs of mental failure. The KCIA saw his usefulness was drawing to a close. He had done a great run—and so had the Korean agents he had kept close to him. His operation continued for over sixty years! I'm guessing they wanted to control the end game rather than watch it run out of its own accord."

"So the KCIA killed all three people?"

"They had the most to gain from doing so."

"What about the money?"

"You mean the supposed nine hundred million US dollars?"

"Everyone seems to know the stakes. Yes, I do."

"Everything's mortgaged at least once over. There's no pot of gold. It's gone."

"So all the infighting about money is a tempest in a teapot?"

"Not exactly. It's still a deadly game. Some of the greatest fortunes in America have ended up being façades. Once the motive power of money is gone, the question is not whether the money will last but when it will finally run out. I'm telling you the Anderson money has run its course. All the interest in the last will and testament is so much wishful thinking."

Fulghum thought about this for a moment. He knew at least three million dollars were real. They were sequestered in numbered accounts. He had access to one of those accounts already. He might get a chance to access the other two, didn't he?

"I can guess what you're thinking. Forget it. It's all fools' gold, John." The CIA agent sat forward in his chair doing his best to sound convincing.

"So why are you here tonight, Ken?"

"I came to tell you to watch your back."

"Who's coming for me, Ken - CIA? KCIA? DPRK?"

"We're trying to assess that now."

"Let me try to put this in my own words." He took a drag on his Marlboro. "I'm effectively becoming your Judas goat. I'm being given the bait to bring the tiger. When the bad guys strike at me, you'll know who they are. You don't know now, or you'd take care of business and not bother me with the classified details. Am I close? Or can't you tell me because I lack a clearance and the need to know?"

"The answers are yes, and yes. If I knew the threat, I would take it out in a heartbeat. Forget the clearance and need to know. I frankly don't know who we're dealing with."

'What do you want me to do?"

"I want you to drive to Pittsfield and somehow team up with our friend Nigel Pounce. Play textbook detective—be Christie's Belgian detective Hercule Poirot—until the killer reveals his or her hand. Help us catch this menace."

"You really think the threat goes farther than to the principal victims - the Judge, his Korean wife, and his lawyer? What would be the point of going further?"

"Some intelligence will get you killed just for knowing it exists. The Koreans on both sides are thorough when they wipe out the traces of their former operations. They can't be sure who knows what, so they kill anyone who might know anything. For example, somehow Nigel Pounce pried up a marble inset to the back entrance of the Judge's estate in Pittsfield. He discovered notebooks with accounts of assassinations. Our analysts are working feverishly on those documents now. They'd like to have the documents that preceded the ones Pounce found. I happen to think those are in the possession of Kim Su Baek right now. She's being watched while she drives down the Mass Pike. She'll be here tomorrow morning if she's lucky. She'll meet you in the back of Joe's Malt Shop at noon. Don't be surprised that I know. This is mission essential knowledge. You and Sue can run, John, but you can't hide when the stakes are this high."

"Okay, Ken. I'm going to meet Sue tomorrow at noon. What is our best next move?"

"Pick up where you left off in New York City. Become her knight in shining armor again. Take your courtly lady back to Pittsfield. Shack up with her at night while during the daylight hours you help Nigel find the killer. Enlist her help if you can. Keep her enthralled and under control if you can't."

"So she becomes my assistant temporarily while we sort things out. Will the deal struck by the Agency and the Chief of Police hold no matter what?"

"You tell me, pal. For all we know, Sue may be the perpetrator after all. We can't ever know how deeply the DPRK has penetrated the KCIA. She could be working for the opposition even though we think her ancestors were squarely on our side. But were they? We'll probably never know."

"Are the boundaries between North and South Korea really that porous?"

"Bet on it. They're all family. Kim is the last name of the current leader of the DPRK. It's also the family name for Anderson's employees. Coincidentally, it's a name held by a third of the Korean people on both sides of the Demilitarized Zone. Look, I've read transcripts indicating the most sensitive sites in the South are fully penetrated by the North. I've read other transcripts of conversations between North Korean political and military figures that could only have been obtained by agents in place."

"Will you and your people be giving us cover all the time we're in Pittsfield?"

"We'll be there, John, but we aren't infallible. You and Pounce dropped off our radar screen when you went fishing in Onota Lake. We picked you up again when you dropped Pounce off at the pier. If something had happened while you were trolling through the water, we weren't in a position to do anything to help you."

Fulghum pondered this for a moment. He lit another Marlboro and asked, "Was Anderson's lawyer one of your people?"

"He was a long-time Agency stringer, too straight-laced and tight-assed to become an agent."

"And he died somehow."

"That's right. We missed an opportunity. Mea culpa. It hurts to know you were right when no one in authority listened."

"Was the lawyer involved in the Judge's operations at any level?"

"He was merely a lawyer, a human messenger service, and faithful scribe. He was Harvard all the way up, a good stick. I hope we nail the man or woman who killed him. You can help us."

"I'm serving Kim Su Baek, Ken. She's my client. I've been hired by her to find the murderer of her father and mother. If incidentally, I find the murderer of the old man's lawyer so much the better for all of us."

"We have an understanding, then, my friend. Do what you do best. Snoop and wait. We'll be watching. If I can help, I'll be in touch. If you find the bad guys are dropping dead around you, it's probably us keeping the fleas off you and Sue. I'm going to have one more finger of JD then I'm off. Believe it or not, this Anderson business is not the only job I'm on right now. The Agency never sleeps, and I don't either."

Ken savored his last finger of whiskey. Then he left the building and disappeared into the night. Fulghum drove home to get some sleep before he saw Sue again. He knew that once they were together, they were likely to be working night and day. He smiled as he remembered the night she dropped her robe and revealed her golden body in all its naked glory.

He said out loud to himself, "The things a man does for God and country." Beside the highway, he saw a buck and a doe just standing tall by the side of the road. He knew they were paralyzed by the headlights, but he saw them as a statuesque tableau, meaning what? Perhaps they were a momentary show of nobility before the traffic passed and they continued their nocturnal feast in darkness.

Chapter 5

The Interrogation of Freddie Hill

"Unfortunately, rice plants soak up arsenic like a sponge. In fact, while all plants absorb some arsenic from the soil, rice plants absorb 20 TIMES more arsenic than other grains. And because organic rice soaks up arsenic from the soil just as greedily as conventional rice, heading to Whole Foods isn't going to save you!"
— Nutrient Insider e-letter, Advanced Bionutritionals, Norcross, Georgia, 2016

Kim Su Baek sat at a small table in the back of Joe's Malt Shop sipping a fountain Coca-Cola through a straw. She was wearing her dark glasses. Her legs were crossed. Her loose foot moved up and down nervously. On the floor by her chair was a suitcase and next to it a leather bag with a shoulder strap. Fulghum had just joined her as they had planned.

"It's good to see you. Did you have a pleasant trip?"

"John, I'm tired. I drove all through the night. I'd like to find a safe place, shower, and sleep for the rest of the day. My car across the street has a ticket on the windshield. A strange man is watching, so I'm avoiding it."

"Why don't I drive you to my place? You can shower there and get some sleep. When you feel up to it, we're going back to Pittsfield."

"I just got out of there again. Why would I want to go back?"

"We're going back to catch your father's murderer."

"Can't you go back alone and leave me at your apartment?"

"That wouldn't be a good idea. You're in danger. I need to keep you close for your own safety. I'll also need to have you interpret what's happening in the investigation at the estate."

"I brought a sample notebook from the safe deposit box in Seoul. It's in the bag on the floor next to my suitcase." She touched the bag by way of illustration. "I placed the other notebooks in a new box at a different bank in Seoul. The notebook I brought is the last in the series by date. I can explain it to you when you like."

"Sue, the police found the cache of notebooks under the marble slab at the estate. A team of experts is working with them now."

She laughed. "John, the police will never be able to decipher those documents."

"I'm inclined to agree, but the team is not from the police."

"You're telling me the CIA is involved now?"

"Is it surprising? Are you finished with your Coke?"

"Yes. We can go now."

"You're going to take my arm. We'll take the back way out and walk to my car. Now stand up. I'll carry your suitcase. You bring the bag with the notebook. Let's go."

The couple left the malt shop by the rear exit and found Fulghum's car parked behind it. He quickly checked the vehicle for any signs of tampering. Then he put the luggage in the trunk. They climbed in, and he drove her to his apartment.

While she showered, the detective paged through the notebook. The text was in Hangul except for the dates and a few names spelled out in Roman script. He found a yellow pad and a pencil. He copied the names and dates. When Sue emerged from the bathroom, she wore a plain cotton tunic with her hair tied in a towel. She walked up to him and laid her hand on his shoulder.

"John, I'm going to go back to your bed and sleep. I won't be setting an alarm. I see you found the notebook and written some names. Other names are in Hangul. I'll help you decipher the text after my nap."

She stumbled back to his bedroom and closed the door behind her. Fulghum silenced his cell phone. Since he would need Sue's help to decipher the notebook, he decided to clean his .38 police special pistol while she was sleeping. He took off his shoulder holster and laid it on the table. He fetched his rag and gun oil and a box of ammunition. Though his office might be a mess, Fulghum was always careful to keep his firearms in pristine condition. He efficiently unloaded, cleaned and oiled his gun. He found it ironical he had recently visited his makeshift shooting range in the field in Milford but only to burn documents. He carefully reloaded his weapon and was about to reinsert it in his holster when he heard someone tinkering with his front door.

Shots were fired, and Fulghum's door was splintered near the lock assembly. He rolled to the floor as two men kicked his door open and came inside firing their weapons. He shot the lead man in the head. When the man's follower pulled his gun towards where Fulghum was lying, the detective shot the man in the shoulder of his shooting arm. The man kept coming, pulling another gun with his left hand. Fulghum coolly shot him in the head before he could take aim.

Fulghum heard movement and a gasp behind him. He wheeled and trained his weapon. He did not shoot because he saw Sue standing in the doorway to his bedroom with one hand over her mouth. In her other hand was a small pistol aimed at the front door. A third man barged into the apartment with his gun drawn. Sue shot him once in the heart and once in the head.

"Sue, I'm going to dial 911 now. Give me your gun. I want you to get dressed quickly. Take my keys and drive my car around the area randomly. Be sure to take your phone with you. I'll call you when it's clear for you to return."

"Yes, this is John Fulghum reporting attempted murder by three persons at my residence. All three entered my apartment with weapons drawn and firing. They are all now dead on my living room floor. I'm calling from Apartment 109, East Lake Village Apartments, Bedford. You have my cell phone number from Caller ID. I'll be here waiting for the first responders."

"These three men are all Korean," Sue exclaimed as she opened her suitcase. While she dressed, she said, "They were a hit team sent to kill us. They must have followed us here."

"Here are my keys. Wear your dark glasses. Go straight to my car and drive. The emergency folks will be here in minutes. Leave your bags here. I'll keep them safe."

Sue took his keys, walked over the bodies and out the shattered door. Fulghum closed her suitcase and lugged it to his bedroom closet. He hid the bag with the notebook in the overhead crawl space. Sue had been gone for three minutes when the emergency team plus two black and whites arrived with their flashing lights and sirens on. The police climbed out of their vehicles with their weapons drawn and fanned out to assure the shooting was truly over. One policeman, followed by two paramedics, ran into the building and gingerly stepped over the bodies in Fulghum's living room. There they found the detective standing and holding his identification high with one hand and the other raised where they could see it. His weapon and Sue's lay on the table.

"I'm the one who dialed 911," he said. Pointing to the three intruders, he said, "These are the men who tried to kill me."

The policeman lowered his weapon and checked Fulghum's identification. He then made a call to the station. He told the paramedics, "Check these three men for signs of life but leave them exactly where they are. We don't want to contaminate the scene."

Fulghum's cell phone rang. Caller ID indicated Nigel Pounce was the caller.

"Officer, I'm just getting a call from the chief of homicide. May I take it?"

"Go ahead."

"Hello, Nigel. Has news traveled fast, or is your call coincidental to attempted murder?"

"John, are you okay?"

"I'm fine. I can't say the same for the three corpses lying in my living room."

"Please give your phone to the officer in charge so I can talk with him."

"Officer Sweeny, Officer Pounce would like to talk with you on this line."

Sweeny took Fulghum's phone and stepped outside the apartment. Fulghum saw Sweeny register the lead paramedic's horizontal head movement indicating they had found no signs of life in any of the three bodies.

When Sweeny came back to return Fulghum's cell phone, he said, "Officer Pounce vouches for you, so everything must be okay. We're going to scour everything that might allow us to identify who these killers are. Gathering the evidence will take time."

For the next three hours, the police and first responders collected statements and evidence. Fulghum wrote a statement and signed it. Police photographers documented the scene. Police went apartment by apartment to collect information about what people had seen and heard. They found the automobile in which the three murderers came. They called in a tow truck and impounded the car.

Finally, the paramedics were allowed to bag and drag the three corpses to the emergency vehicle for transport to police forensics and then the city morgue. Before he departed, Sweeny secured and collected the weapons plus shell casings that littered the floor of the apartment.

Sweeny told Fulghum, "I guess it will be all right for you to call the people who can put your residence back in order now. If you can think of anything you haven't written in your deposition that could be of interest, please give me a call." He handed Fulghum his card.

"Thanks, officer. I'll do that." He glanced over the card and placed it in his shirt pocket.

Fulghum gave the police and paramedics ten minutes from the time they had departed before he called Sue to say the coast was clear for her return. He then called the apartment manager and told her he would need a new front door and door sill as soon as possible. He said he'd also need cosmetic work done for the places bullets had damaged the interior of his apartment. When Sue arrived, a work crew was busy making repairs while the apartment manager supervised. Fulghum told the manager he was going to go to his office for a couple of hours.

"Go right ahead, Mr. Fulghum. By the time you return, your door will be fixed and your interior patched up. Stop by the office for your new door key. If I'm not around then, my son Marty will give you the key. It looks like you're lucky to be alive."

"That's about right, Mrs. Sampson. Thanks for getting right on with the repairs. I'll see you later."

Mrs. Sampson watched Sue with curiosity all the way to Fulghum's car. Fulghum waved to her through the window wondering whether she would want to raise his rate now that he had a new friend visiting.

"You must have been bored to distraction driving for three and a half hours."

"The New England countryside is beautiful in the sunshine. I drove out to Gloucester Point and watched the sea."

"Did you have any new thoughts about our visitors? By the way, you did some nice shooting. It was very professional."

"In reverse order, John. Thank you for the compliment. It pays for a girl to know how to defend herself in these times. I've been thinking about the killers. Two broke through the door and rushed into the room, one to each side, high and low. The third man didn't enter until he thought the shooting was over. He may have been the driver of their car."

"Did anything about their entry seem familiar to you?"

"What do you mean?"

"Do you know how an assassination team operates?"

"John, my ancestors were civilized. They didn't run around shooting people. They killed quietly, with poison in tea. They never disturbed the neighbors with violence and noise." She seemed offended by his insinuation.

"Was there any way of telling whether the victims were from the North or the South?"

"I'm going to guess they were from the North."

"What makes you think so?"

"Their clothes and shoes had poor workmanship. I think your police forensic team will discover they are agents of North Korea. If so, they won't be the last to try to kill us."

"I hate to disillusion you, but the police are unlikely to care about anything but the violence of their entry and their evident intent to kill me."

"Only you?"

"As far as my deposition stated, only me."

"Will you give me back my pistol?"

Fulghum reached into the inside pocket of his jacket and fetched out her gun, which he put on safe and handed to her.

"Thank you. You told your apartment manager we were going to your office. Are we going there?"

"Yes. We've got a lot to catch up on. I thought we'd avoid getting in the way of the workers putting my place back together. We don't have the notebook—it's hidden in my apartment."

"I hope it's well hidden."

"We'll see. Do you want a salad or sandwich?"

"I'm starving. Yes, let's eat."

They stopped at a Subway and picked up two salads plus soft drinks which they took to eat in Fulghum's office. While they ate, Fulghum asked Sue for details of her trip to Seoul.

"I flew from New York to Seoul. I stayed only long enough to obtain the notebooks and to place all but one in another bank's repository. I decided to fly back to Boston Logan rather than New York because you are here."

"I suppose you didn't count on being apprehended when you landed?"

"The authorities were a little more efficient than I thought."

"Not efficient enough to seize the notebook you were carrying?"

"I think not. I was lucky."

"Okay. Then the police drove you to Pittsfield?"

"Yes," she said, eating another bite of salad and sipping her drink. She smiled. "When I arrived, Officer Pounce said he wanted to interrogate me."

"Did that happen?"

"Interrogation in America is a lot different from interrogation in Korea."

"I'll bet. No whips nor shock treatment. No shouting and teams of badgers day and night."

"Is that what Americans think of as Korean justice?"

"What did you tell Officer Pounce?"

"I told him I was willing to help him find the real murderer. I said I'd hired you to help me do that. We only talked for about half an hour."

"Then what happened?"

"Officer Pounce received a telephone call. His face changed. When the call was over, he told me he had no further questions for me. He said I was free to go."

"Do you know who called him?"

"I don't know, and I don't really care. I left the estate immediately. Now I'm here." She held out her arms as a demonstration of the fact.

"Let's take a little time to consider all the employees at the estate and each person who had frequent contact there. Relax and talk. Maybe the best way to start is for you to tell me everything you remember about the day before your mother had her symptoms."

"The first thing to happen that day was Freddie Hill."

"Who's he?"

"He's the Judge's prodigal favorite grand-nephew Frederick Hamblin 'Freddie' Hill, one of the vultures who was always hanging around the estate waiting for his grand-uncle to die. He stayed at the estate while trying to work out what to do with his life. He's a rake and a gambler. He has enormous gambling debts yet still plays the horses regularly."

"There's nothing wrong with playing the horses," Fulghum asserted. "I play the horses too. These are racing forms there on the floor against the walls of this office."

"You don't go around pinching my bottom like Freddie does."

"Not unless you ask me to pinch you, I don't." He smiled.

"You're not at all like Freddie. He's borrowed extensively against his future trust earnings. Of all the family who stays at the estate, he's the one person who'd have gained most by his grand-uncle's death."

"Excuse me while I make a call."

She nodded and continued eating her salad.

Fulghum speed dialed Nigel Pounce's number and left a message on his voicemail. "Nigel, this is John. Have you interrogated Freddie Hill about his debts against future earnings of trust funds of the Judge's estate? Give me a call about that when you get the chance."

"So we're helping with the investigation?"

"Why not? It's one way of narrowing the field of suspects, isn't it? Besides, if we're going to bring the murderers to justice, we can't wait for them to come shooting their way through our door."

She shuddered and looked down. "We had a close call today, didn't we?"

"The more I dwell on it, the more I'm convinced I was their target, not you."

"Why do you say that?"

"The first two came through the door looking to encounter opposition by me. They hoped to shoot me. What bothered me about the third man was his fixation on me. He didn't seem to countenance you when you entered the room even though you had your gun trained on him. In retrospect, it seems he thought you didn't matter. Or put another way, he didn't consider you a threat. If I had been in his shoes, I would have shot you dead before I aimed at me. If he had done that, we both would've been lying on that floor. He would have escaped. We wouldn't be sitting here eating lunch and talking about the suspects."

"So what scenario do you envision for what happened?"

"I don't know yet. I have a hunch. That's all."

"Why don't you eat your lunch? The salad's very good. The lettuce is crispy. If you wait, the salad dressing will make it limp."

Fulghum took a couple of bites of salad. Then he sat upright. "I've got an idea. Why didn't I think of it before?"

"You needed nourishment?"

"Pardon me while I make another call."

He speed dialed Silvia's number. When his call went to her voicemail, he said, "Silvia, this is John. Can you give me the real names and contact data for either Currier or Ives? Just leave a message if I don't answer. Ciao."

"So in the middle of our discussions about murder, you're interested in antiquarian prints?"

"Something like that, Sue. We may be heading to western Massachusetts soon, so I want to cover a few bases out here before we leave. Tell me everything you associate with the Korean word Arirang."

"It's the national anthem of South Korea. I associate it with beauty. The music for the song penetrates the soul. It is also the name for an annual athletic competition in the DPRK. There it's a context for socialist propaganda glorifying the Kim regime."

"Your name is Kim. Are you related to the clan in the north?"

"John, there are many Kims in Korea. All Kims are distantly related. My people are from the royal offshoots. We shouldn't be compared with the socialist savages in the current regime."

"I'm going to ask you a difficult question. Don't get insulted, please. Can you tell the difference between a North Korean and a South Korean? If so, what differentiates them?"

"That's an interesting question. I have friends who spend all their time worrying about how to tell them apart because it's their job to do so. They work in the counterintelligence service."

"By that do you mean the KCIA?"

"How do you know about that? Never mind. Yes, they are KCIA agents."

"So what do they look for?"

"They look for distinctions without a difference, John."

"You'll have to explain that for me."

"It's easy to tell by the anger or fanaticism in the eyes, the rake-thin and wiry bodies, the studious brutality of those who have been reared in the North. The trouble is the enemy has studied the South and Westerners enough to shape their agents, so they blend right into their surroundings."

"So the usual distinctions would disappear. Perhaps only by a slip of the tongue or a look which betrays them could you discern who they are?"

"The signs are highly technical."

"Will you explain that?"

"In the North, they have had breeding experiments for many decades. Americans who were taken prisoner were bred with Korean women. Their offspring were raised as Westerners in special camps in the North. They were subjected to surgery and special classes to train them to infiltrate the United States under assumed identities. When you copied down the names from the notebook I brought back from Korea, you wrote names of some of those sleeper agents. My grandmother and mother were used to hunt them down and kill them before they completed their missions against your country."

"They must have had excellent intelligence to know those agents' names."

"Yes, and all such intelligence about DPRK agents in America flowed through Stephen Anderson. When I first came to know of these things from my family, I thought my father was a god, all knowing and all seeing. He received information from couriers who stayed at the estate briefly. They brought intelligence and orders from the South. He gave them intelligence and operational reports about the assassinations my people carried out. The notebooks are shorthand accounts of those assassinations."

"Experts say it's hard to tell the allegiance of agents on either side of the Demilitarized Zone. What do you think about that idea?"

"The experts are right. The reason is simple. Both sides want Korea to be reunified. We are all one big family, after all. You've heard our nation was once called the Hermit Kingdom. We stood for ourselves against all outsiders - Chinese, Japanese and all Westerners. The DPRK continues the tradition fanatically."

"You sound as if you approve of their position."

"It's hard not to admire juche, what you would call self-reliance, yet Ralph Waldo Emerson extolled that quality as a virtue. So see what I mean, John. It's very hard to find a difference which has a clear distinction. Koreans are like a dysfunctional family. We'll kill each other en masse, but we'll stand against all outsiders in the end. Germans in Europe are the same."

"External threats cause unity on a temporary basis, but when the threats cease, the factions tear the unity apart."

"Exactly."

They contemplated this enigma for a few moments. Then Fulghum received a call from Pounce.

"Hi, Nigel. Are you returning my voicemail?"

"What possessed you to bring up Freddie Hill today? The man's just been murdered."

"How did he die?" Fulghum asked as he switched his phone to speaker and held a finger to his lips to keep Sue quiet.

"We had scheduled his interrogation in the Judge's study in two parts. This morning was the first part. Hill broke down and confessed his desire to kill his great-uncle but not to the killing itself. He spelled out how he accumulated his enormous debts saying the Korean mafia was behind the loans. The way he put it, Korean women handle the money for the community, but the men are the enforcers. He was being plagued by the enforcers, holding them off by promises of repayment when he received his inheritance."

"That all makes sense. You said you planned a second interrogation."

"It was scheduled for two o'clock this afternoon. When he failed to show up, I sent Riley to Hill's room. Hill was lying on his back in the middle of his bed. He wasn't breathing. Riley dialed 911. The medics came at once, but found no vital signs in Hill. He was declared dead on arrival at the emergency room. He succumbed exhibiting the same symptoms as the Judge. I ordered an autopsy. We'll have to wait for the results. I fear we have another case of arsenic poisoning. Absent a suicide note, he is therefore eliminated as a suspect in the other poisonings, but everyone on the estate is again a suspect in his murder."

"Ouch. This seems like a nightmare plague, only it's poison and not microbes doing the killing. I suppose the timing exonerates Kim Su Baek?"

"Yes, on the surface of things, it does exonerate her. Speaking of killing, I'm glad you could defend yourself. I've gotten a preliminary report about the three gunmen who tried to kill you. Guess what?"

"No ID, no prints on file, no trace on their weapons?"

"Right on all counts and there's more. Our favorite Agency stepped in to curtail any further investigation. They confiscated the bodies and flew them out—to one of their black anatomy theaters most probably. We'll never hear what they discover from their forensic analysis. You should be glad to know you're in the clear. You may not want to tell me who your backup shooter was. I don't care. You were lucky, my friend."

"What about the trust funds?"

"We found among the grandnephew's effects a portfolio of documents with all prior versions of his uncle's wills and trust documents. Evidently, the Judge changed these documents frequently according to whim. The latest documents in Freddie's portfolio were much more generous to him than the documents that the lawyer's partner claimed superseded them."

"What was the date of the latest will in the portfolio?"

"It was executed in the month of May seven years ago. That version left everything to Hill, who was described as 'my favorite grand-nephew.' Against that was built a scaffold of debt that will astound you."

"Except the whole financial edifice has all come tumbling down. Someone must be glad it happened. I know the money lenders can't be very unhappy."

"Unless his death was caused by them. Look, I've got to get back to my interrogations. Keep the ideas coming. FYI, I'm no closer to a solution now than when we last talked. Thanks for your continued inputs. It would be great to have you out here for nightly debriefings, maybe out on the water. Don't feel pressured. Goodbye for now." Pounce terminated the call on his end.

"Well, Sue, you are off the hook for Hill's death."

"Perhaps, but not for the others - if anyone wants to bring me back into the picture."

"What do you know about the trust funds? They seem to be on a separate track from the wills."

'The trusts are the corpus of the estate, with notable exceptions. They were established decades ago when there were thirteen children and my father wanted to protect his legacy from his brothers' and sisters' plundering."

"What were the notable exceptions?"

"You may remember from your childhood hearing the tales of the Arabian nights?"

"Vividly."

"You'll remember accounts of fabulous caves filled with gold, silver, precious jewels and pearls."

"Where are you heading with this?"

"My father believed governments can take everything away that they can seize."

"And your point is . . ."

"My point is, he sequestered a lot of his wealth in untraceable assets and squirreled them away in unlikely places."

"So, like the documents he hid under the marble on the back entrance, he built something like the Cavern of the Forty Thieves that Ali Baba rifled."

"Only there is no 'open sesame' to open the door. There's more."

"I'm listening. I'm also fascinated. Go on."

"My father placed his treasures all over the world. He also played with cryptocurrencies like Bitcoin."

"That has to be very recent—since 2012. Your mother wouldn't have known about that development."

"He asked me to look into cryptocurrencies for him and manage a separate experimental portfolio. He pooled Bitcoin before the big run up in value to twelve hundred dollars. Then he sold everything and crashed the market before having me invest everything in small lots again at between one hundred and two hundred fifty. We sold out again when the price hit four hundred twenty. We made a fortune that was totally invisible to outsiders. My father called me his Cryptocurrency Queen. That's of course nonsense because he guided all the investments. I just found the way for him to invest his money and juggle it. I might have done better work for him because I was still working my way through college and graduate school at the time."

Fulghum's phone rang before he could ask his next question.

"Look, I have a question about that, but it'll have to wait while I take this call. Excuse me."

Fulghum stood up, walked out his door and down the stairwell while he answered the call from Silvia.

"This is Silvia. John, where are you?"

"Hi, Silvia. Thanks for returning my call. I'm near my office."

"I'm relieved. Your neighborhood has been the subject of radio reports all afternoon. Three men were killed in a shootout in your apartment complex. I was worried you might be involved."

"Don't worry. I survived. The men who came to kill me did not. I'm not in the least sorry they died."

"Oh, John! Why are you always getting into these situations?"

"Just be glad they didn't burst in on us the other night. Are you all right?"

"I'm fine, John. I just worry about you all the time."

"Me too. Anyway, please watch your back for both our sakes. Did you dredge up anything on Currier and Ives?"

"You're going to have to move fast. Currier died five years ago of terminal cancer. Ives is in a nursing home in Needham under the name Clancy Frew. That's his pseudonym. He's written over one hundred westerns with that name as the author. I made a call to Needham Pastures. He can receive visitors. Do you want me to meet you there? His visiting hours are between ten and three, with a break for lunch between eleven and one."

"Let's set up a meeting at ten o'clock. I'm going to bring another person to the meeting."

"I'll bet she's your new friend Sue. Am I right? Well, from your silence, I'll guess I'm right. I'd like to meet her. I really would. See you both at ten tomorrow. Be there or be square."

"Silvia, be nice in the sandbox."

"Don't worry. I won't punch her lights out while you're watching." She laughed wickedly and terminated the call.

Fulghum saw a tow truck backing up to take Sue's car away. He went up to the driver and said, "Wait a minute. What do you need to forget about towing this vehicle?"

"I don't know what you mean, mister," she said. "I've got a towing order. This vehicle is going to the Bedford pound. With proper identification and one hundred dollars, he can bail it out and do whatever."

"It's a beautiful day. What if the car wasn't here when you arrived to tow it away? What then?"

"How can a car just disappear like that?" she asked, with a wily smile.

He held up a hundred-dollar bill. "Hocus pocus dominocus," he intoned.

She grabbed the hundred and smiled. "I see what you mean. I mean, I don't see any car here. Of course, if I come again and discover it's returned, I'll just have to tow it. So I'll check in two hours. If it continues to elude my gaze, I'll report it has having been reclaimed by the owner. It's happened before. Of course, I'll have to split the hundred to be sure."

Fulghum knew where her conversation was heading.

"Look, what's your name?"

"Sondra Fleming, that's Sondra with an O."

"Well, Sondra with an O, would two Jacksons help in this situation?"

"Better make it quick. Soon it'll be Tubmans."

"You are so right. She was a gun toting chick, a real badass dame."

"A lesson for us all," Sondra said with a broad smile opening her vest to reveal her concealed weapon. Fulghum handed her the two twenties. Then as she drove her tow truck away, he looked around and skipped up the stairs to his office.

"Sue, bring your purse. While the coast is clear, we're going to reposition your vehicle. I sure hope it'll start."

Sue climbed in and inserted her key. The engine turned over without a hiccup. She drove the car to the back of Joe's Malt Shop then came through the rear entry of the eatery. She met Fulghum out front and went back up to his office. Fulghum noticed she had in her hand the ticket that had been slipped under her windshield wiper. He held out his trash can so she could file it appropriately.

"We're going to have to find a place to store your car while we take our summer vacation in the Berkshires. Before we depart tomorrow, we're going to pay a visit to an elderly scribbler in a nursing home in Needham. I hope you're game to go. I'd also like you to meet one of my oldest friends."

"Is your friend female?"

"As a matter of fact, she is. I hope you'll be able to play nice in the sandbox."

"I promise I won't kill her, if that's what you mean."

"Maiming, injuring and threatening are also out."

"She must be very special to you."

"Yes, Sue, she is. She is also very special to you though you don't yet realize it."

"How's that?"

"I think she holds the key to the mystery we're trying to solve."

"Can you be more specific?"

"At this stage, I can't. It's only a feeling I have."

"You sound like my grandmother."

"Was your grandmother's intuition largely right?"

"John, my grandmother was never wrong about a feeling. So I'll give this person a break. I'll know when I meet her whether she's going to be what you say she is."

Fulghum began to dread the very meeting he had set up. Perhaps he should tell Sue to stay at his apartment while he and Silvia went to see Frew. Then he had another feeling that excluding her would lose an opportunity.

The couple talked about the other denizens of the estate until after nightfall. Then they drove in tandem to his apartment complex. He retrieved the new key to his home from his apartment manager's son.

"Your place is as good as new, Mr. Fulghum. You must be a dead shot to have killed all three of those murdering scum. The good thing from my mother's point of view was the publicity. No one will forget what happened here today. The bad thing from my point of view is the rep your gun fighting skills gave this neighborhood. Fort Apache in the Bronx comes to mind. I had three offers for your apartment from known drug dealers late this afternoon. I knew you'd be back, so I refused deals they thought I couldn't refuse. Anyway, I hope you like the fix-up. Mom asked whether your lady friend would be your companion from now on. She thinks a rate adjustment might be in order."

Sue's eyes widened at this prospect. Fulghum said, "We're only here to pick up her things. She was storing them temporarily in my place while she got her life in order. She's staying in a motel tonight and driving out to western Massachusetts tomorrow midday. Tell Mom it's going to be okay—until the next bunch of scumbags arrives to get me."

Fulghum laughed. The boy laughed and winked, leaning his head towards Sue with a leer. She scowled daggers at both men and folded her arms with a huff.

"This place reeks of testosterone," she muttered. The boy laughed harder when he heard her comment.

Fulghum turned the key in the new lock of his apartment. His new door and jamb were white oak of demonstration quality. His apartment's interior never looked better. There was no sign that anything untoward had happened earlier in the day. Fulghum checked out the places where bullets had become embedded in the walls and the forensic crew had dug them out. He couldn't tell that the walls had been re-plastered and repainted. Sue walked through the place and sat down on the bed.

"Except for a faint smell of drying paint, I'd say you got an upgrade with all the options." She laughed. "Maybe you should order in assassins on a regular basis, perhaps including some to do a shootout at your office."

"Sue, I've already tried that at my office. You saw the 'after' version there."

"There it didn't have the je ne sais quoi. Too bad. Anyway, what are we going to do now?"

"We're going to stow your car in long term parking somewhere and find a motel where you can shower and get some rest, so you're presentable tomorrow bright and early."

"Merde."

"Et merde encoure. Tough, Sue. We're going to be fresh for tomorrow and ready for a long day's journey into night. I know just where we'll camp out in Pittsfield. You'll like it."

"Are you slinking off to visit your female friend and leave me all alone?"

"No. I'm leaving you all alone to visit a male friend."

"That's kinky."

"Perhaps, but it may save your life tomorrow."

"All right. Don't blame me for not liking that you'll not be here pleasuring me." Pouting, she raised her face in his direction. Fulghum pulled her in close and kissed her long and hard until she melted in his arms.

"Oh, John, since New York, I've thought of you constantly."

"Sue, tonight when we reach the motel, get some sleep. I mean it. I'll pick you up at nine thirty for our trip to the rest facility."

"That early? I'll have to set my alarm for seven to be fully ready."

"So what? The man we're going to see got the closest to your father while he was in uniform. I want you to look like a million bucks. That way, you'll bring back memories we need to solve our mystery. Do you understand me?"

"You know I look radiant after we've made glorious, passionate love all night."

"That's not the glow you'll need tomorrow. I need for you to look like your father's intellectual child. I want this man to look into your eyes and see your father, not some moonstruck courtesan who's been the subject of a randy man's rutting through the night."

"John, sometimes you have all the charm of a warthog."

"Thank you, Sue. I won't return the compliment. I will, however, say thank you for being Annie Oakley today. You saved my life. I won't forget it."

She stood tall, and for a moment, he saw something in her eyes he had not seen before - a quiet pride, the kind of look that must have characterized her father in his early days. Fulghum knew now his choice of having her attend the meeting with Frew was right on target. He kissed her on the cheek.

"Let's be sure we have everything before we go."

He retrieved her suitcase and opened the compartment where he had stashed the notebook. They went out of the apartment, and he locked the door. In the parking area, he loaded their baggage into his trunk.

He told Sue where they would be driving and asked her to keep her cell phone handy in case they encountered trouble. Then they drove off, with Fulghum leading.

They dropped her car at an airport long term parking facility and found a Residence Inn in Needham. There Fulghum saw to it that she was settled in their suite and kissed Sue goodbye. He kept the keys to her car in his pocket just for luck.

"I might be back before daylight, but in any case, I'll pick you up at nine thirty in the morning for the quick trip to the long-term care facility."

Sue was not consoled. Resigned to a night alone in a strange place, she decided to make the best of the situation. She took a long, luxurious bath and afterward put on her gold silk robe with the embroidered cranes. She set her alarm for seven o'clock and sat in bed leafing page by page through the notebook that detailed her father's assassinations. She tried to discern patterns in her great-grandmother's and grand-mother's activities but finally fell asleep.

Meanwhile, Fulghum drove to the Needham Dunkin' Donuts and met Ken Mander as he had suggested in a voicemail message earlier in the day. Fulghum knew he had, once again, been drawn into the Agency's dark web of associations. He did not know where the vectors were going to point him next, but he went into the Agency's bewildering maze anyway. Though not an agent or even an Agency stringer, when the call to service came, Fulghum always answered it.

Chapter 6

The Interrogation of Cecily Portius

"Two North Korean defectors and former spies say Cold War-type missions are ongoing. One claims that hundreds of the communist nation's agents are in the U.S. at any given time." — http://www.washingtontimes.com/news/2015/may/22/hundreds-north-korean-spies-us-any-given-time-defe/

Fulghum drove into the parking area of the Dunkin' Donuts in Needham, and Ken Mander pulled into the space right beside his. Mander got out of his vehicle and climbed into the passenger side of Fulghum's car. Fulghum pulled into traffic and headed for the highway.

"Let's drive for a while, John. It's a beautiful, balmy night. Do you know the University Avenue stop on the AMTRAK route?"

Fulghum nodded.

"Well, head for that. I don't know about you, but I need a smoke."

Fulghum reached for his box of Marlboro Reds and gave a cigarette to Mander. The detective treated himself to another. They lit up and simultaneously rolled down their windows an inch.

Mander was silent for a while. Then he said, "John, I'm glad you survived to fight another day."

"I thought you had my back." He looked askance at his friend.

"Actually we were working against the same team, but it wasn't only the three who broke through your door. Another team of three from the same source was planning to spoil Pounce's party at the estate in Pittsfield."

"I hope they didn't make as much mess as the men who came for me."

"Fortunately not. My people used a tranquilizer gun on one and killed the other two. The stunned man is now singing under implemented interrogation. The man you know as Rex Mason has a team working on the recordings of what he said."

"So yours were Korean?"

"Yes. DPRK. They were unacknowledged agents on US soil. These agents are highly compartmentalized, so they execute on very limited orders and have no perspective beyond their individual tasks."

"Have you learned anything useful from your interrogation?"

"The six clandestine operatives were sent into Massachusetts one week ago. They were supported by two sleeper agents already in place. The operators worked independently of the spotters for their targets, so we don't know who the spotters are. My men are picking up the two sleepers as I speak. We'll know more after they've been interrogated if all goes well."

"Do the six operatives relate to what happened at the estate in Pittsfield?"

"Oddly, I don't think so. In fact, I believe they're a mop-up team sent in anticipation of actions by another sleeper group under separate leadership."

"The complexity of this espionage design is intriguing, but not very helpful for my purposes."

"We know for certain you and Pounce were targeted by name."

"That's something. Why did we rate top billing?"

"Someone is worried the two of you, working together, will discover something big. Perhaps you already have done so but don't realize it."

"Was Kim Su Baek specifically targeted?"

"Not according to the man we interrogated. He didn't seem to know the name."

"Of course, he may have known her by some other name."

"Now you're thinking like one of us. I'm going by knowledge we actually can verify. I must assume if two teams were sent to kill you both at the same time, others will follow to finish the botched jobs. Again, I urge you go to Pittsfield at your earliest opportunity so we can focus a defense on you and Pounce without becoming too stretched by geography."

"Relax. I'm driving Sue out to Pittsfield tomorrow after a quick and necessary visit."

"Will you tell me about the visit?"

Fulghum chain lit a cigarette and handed Mander another so he could do the same.

"I can do that, but I'd appreciate it if you don't tell your people about it until I've completed the visit and driven to the Mass Pike. Also, I'll need coverage for another person portal to portal."

"Silvia?"

"Yes. Tell Figlear I need protection for Silvia from now until I return to the Greater Boston area. She's in a red sector for reasons that will become clear."

"I can do that."

Fulghum nodded and took a long draft on his cigarette.

"I've seen a file that no longer exists because I burned it. It was comprised of notes by two reporters who interviewed Anderson and others but had their story spiked from on high. Some details in the surviving notes are red hot."

"You have me intrigued. I thought the notebooks were the key to the mystery."

"They're important for the assassinations. They give nothing about why Anderson assumed the role he did. With the notebooks, we have the what. With the notes I read, we potentially have the why. After tomorrow morning I should be able to confirm that."

"So we have two artifacts which may have triggered the hits."

"I think the hits were to be accomplished simultaneously because we hadn't yet put together what Pounce and I had independently discovered. Does that make sense?"

"I need more data before I can decide. Back up a few paces and put me in the picture."

"Pounce found the Korean notebooks under the marble of the back entrance to the estate. I am linked to the rest of the notebooks and to the papers. They may give us insight into the motives. The more I dwell on the details I know, the more I'm convinced the answer to the mystery lies in how those materials integrate into a single picture. Now does that make sense?"

"I get it, but I don't have a clue what the integration of those pieces means."

Fulghum shrugged. "Neither do I. Do you care to brainstorm with me?" Fulghum pulled off the 128 to approach the University Avenue station. He entered the parking area and positioned the car so he could exit quickly in case of emergencies. He left the motor running while they talked.

"I've learned something since we last talked. The Roman script names scattered in the Hangul of the notebooks are the names of DPRK sleeper operatives targeted for assassination by the KCIA."

"That's significant intelligence."

"There's more. Interspersed in the notebooks are the Korean names for those operatives and other operatives who were targeted as well. I'm going to work all this out with my special source, who is the only one alive to help us crack the code. I, therefore, need to have copies of the notebooks Pounce discovered and turned over to your people."

"Do you know what you're asking?"

"I think so. Ken, you work miracles every day. Will you get me those copies?"

"I'll get you those copies if you give me copies of the other notebooks."

"Well, we have a problem. I can possibly give you a copy of one of the other notebooks. The remainder will take some doing."

"I deduce your special source brought you one notebook from her collection but hid the others in a safe place only she can access."

"Anyone would have done the same thing, Ken. She's not only smart. She's got special help."

"Okay, the trade will be your one for my many. Done. What about the roughs from the newspaper reporters you discovered?"

"I can't give you those, but I can give you the gist of their content. If I do that, I must insist you keep the details entirely secret from the Agency."

"That's a turnabout."

"That's the deal."

"All right. Give me the gist. I won't hear it except as deep background."

"Have another cigarette, Ken. Do you have us under surveillance now or are we now off the grid?"

"My people are watching the exit from 128. They're also inside the station watching for the opposition. It's as close as you're going to get to off the grid as we know it."

"Anderson won the Congressional Medal of Honor for successfully destroying a black biological warfare center in North Korea."

"The target had to be black and well protected since the Chinese were all over it."

"They weren't the only ones. The head honcho for the biowar program was a Soviet agent whom Anderson, with the help of the KCIA, kidnapped and delivered alive to the UN forces."

"Wow! You don't mean it?"

"I shit you not. It gets better."

"You have my full attention, John. I'm now worried for both of us and for anyone else who has this information."

"It seems the politicos went bats about the kidnapping. Thought was given to liquidating Anderson and all others who were involved in the extraction of the Soviet agent. Too many people knew, including two reporters who stumbled upon the information when they interviewed Anderson in the hospital where he was convalescing."

"What the hell happened next?"

"A grand deal was struck. Anderson was to get the Congressional Medal of Honor for heroism above and beyond the call of duty. The capture of the Soviet was to be held close pending negotiations for exchanging him for American prisoners of war held by the Chinese and North Koreans. The Korean CIA went ballistic. Anderson went ballistic too. Among the invisible, deniable deals that were struck was a diabolical bargain which you aren't going to believe. It seems so much like bad pulp fiction."

"You dog. You've got me on the edge of my seat with anticipation. What was the deal?"

"Anderson became the lynchpin for countermeasures against DPRK agents operating as assassins and saboteurs within the continental US."

"Hell, you say! Does it mean he was working for us or for the South Koreans?"

"Now you're getting close to something difficult to parse precisely."

"But that's at the heart of what we've got to know."

"Do you recall what Sir Winston Churchill said about Russia?"

"'Russia is a riddle wrapped in a mystery inside an enigma.'"

"For that, you get an A+. Go to the head of the class."

"Keep going, please."

"From my source, I understand it's almost impossible to sort out the North Korean agents from the South Korean agents outside the actual territories of North and South Korea. Further, the North evidently had a program of breeding spies whereby they could produce deep agents who could blend right into their target countries as sleepers. Anderson and the family associated with him for four generations became the connecting link in a strategy designed to ferret out the DPRK agents infiltrating the USA and to bring them to swift justice outside normal channels."

"Fulghum, either you're a madman bewitched by a Korean witch or a consummate genius with the key to unlock a special relationship. I'll wager neither head of state has any knowledge of this agreement."

"I thought we had many unacknowledged black programs. You once told me that. You justified it by telling me about instances of present dangers which could not be challenged by ordinary law or diplomacy. I won't insult you by recounting cases you and I have collaborated on in that line."

"So let me tell it back to you so I can understand what you just said."

"I'm listening."

"A rogue operation has been going full steam for sixty years without acknowledgments. People have been killed as foreign spies on US soil outside the purview of the Presidential Findings process and the FIAB and God only knows what three and four letter agencies, including the CIA and FBI. One man was at the center of that longstanding operation, and he has been murdered. The fallout from his murder is continuing. The planned murders of you and Pounce were part of this design for retribution and cover-up somehow. Does it sum it up?"

"It will do for the moment, but I think there's more. I also think we haven't found the answer to your question about the timing of events. Why was it important to eliminate the lynchpin of this operation now? You asked that early on. I'm convinced the answer to that question will open other doors for us."

"I hate the fact I agreed not to divulge what you just told me. Can't I tell the DDO about it in a special room?"

"Not yet, Ken. I don't think we know enough to take this intelligence up the chain. If it should by any means become public, a firestorm would commence. The whole web of relationships containing the longest continuing war in our time might come apart at once. We have no idea what clandestine operations might be triggered by a front-page story laying out what I've just told you. If I were a reporter with a story this hot, I…"

"You'd be killed, John. And I'd probably be ordered to do the killing. You really do know how to make life hurt."

"Hey, I'm the one whose life is on the line."

"You, and everyone else who touches you, given what you now know."

"All the more reason to give protection to those who are with me."

"In the same fashion as protection was given to Anderson for all these sixty years?"

"Ken, you're making my point. I'm damn close to knowing the why about Anderson. In my gut, I understand where he stood when he was forced to stand down about his capture of the Soviet agent. I also know what he must have felt when his secret, but legitimate daughter walked into his life. He must have felt rejuvenated. I'll bet he was looking forward to a chance at the world record age. Then he was suddenly killed, and someone out there is cheering. I've got to find him or her. I've got to bring the murderer to justice—soon before more deaths accrue."

"You've pulled the whole case inside out for me, John. Congratulations. Now I'm the one who has to ask you, what next? What should I do?"

"Protect my people, Ken, yourself included. Until we solve this case, we're all at risk."

Ken dwelled on this request. He shook his head. "I'll do whatever I can."

"That's all I can ask of you, friend. I'll take you back to the Dunkin' Donuts. You know where I'll be heading. I guess the next time we meet, we'll be in the Berkshires. Do me a favor out there."

"What's that?"

"When Pounce and I decide to do some midnight fishing, let us alone. If we're meant to bring our thoughts together, we'll have to have a context to do just that."

"I'll give you the room, John. Just remember you'll be assuming a tremendous risk by avoiding our surveillance."

"The reward will be worth the risk, Ken. I've learned that the 'too big to fail' adage needs adjustment. My friends and I are 'too small to fail.'"

"If you say so, pal," Mander said doubtfully.

"I do say so." Fulghum released the brake and drove out of the parking area onto the ramp towards the 128. It was a curving ramp which made a vehicle a sitting duck for any sniper properly positioned to take out an unwary driver or his passenger. Fulghum, fortunately, saw the rifle's flash. Instinctively he turned the wheel and screeched to a halt on the side of the ramp. He and Mander hit the deck outside the car as bullets hit it from three directions. Fulghum had his gun out watching for further gunfire. Mander was prepared to shoot as well as he went over the rail. Fulghum ran along the balustrade and leapt over it, running down the incline among the vegetation towards the place where he had seen the original flash. A figure was running towards him, making a scuffling sound in the brush. Fulghum fired twice at the figure, successfully rendering him inoperative. Mander let off a double tap. A man screamed in agony. Mander fired again, and the screaming stopped.

Fulghum thought they had taken out two snipers. He knew there had been a third. He saw alongside the highway a vehicle parked on the apron. On a hunch, he kept low and ran through the brush towards the vehicle. He lingered at the rear of the vehicle in the sumac which grew just below the mowing line. He did not have long to wait. A man carrying a rifle came out of the sumac not ten feet ahead of where he was hiding.

"Stop right there," he said as he aimed his .38 at the center of the man's back. The man's hands rose. Then he ducked, turned and fired blindly. Fulghum returned fire, hitting the man in the chest. He walked up quickly and kicked the man's rifle away. He frisked the man and found a handgun and knife, which he also threw to one side. Keeping the man covered, he asked the man's name. He heard a gurgling sound from the man's bleeding chest wound. Then he heard the unmistakable sound of glass breaking – a sound he had heard before.

"Mander, this one's just broken a suicide capsule. He's a goner. Mander, are you out there?"

"I'm right beside you, pal. The two others had no IDs. I'll wager they used a stolen car. I've got a cleaner crew on the way. You drive on out of here and go back to your suite. I'll stay here and supervise the clean up. Get moving, John. My guys will take me back to the Dunkin' Donuts."

'I'll see if I can get my car started. I've no idea what the sniper shots hit."

"The sooner you get clear, the better. These bozos likely had a report to make within half an hour or so. Whoever doesn't get the report may send another team. When they get here, I'll be ready with a surprise. I don't want the surprise to include you."

Fulghum went back to his car. The windshield had been blown away. Glass was everywhere. Bullet holes stippled the car's exterior. Nevertheless, the wheels were intact, and the car started. Fulghum pulled out on the ramp and continued to the 128. He drove without incident back to the long-term parking lot where he left Sue's car. Fortunately, she had given him her keys. He swapped his car for hers and drove hers back to the motel.

Outside their room, he dusted his clothing to get rid of most of the shattered glass. He inserted the card key and opened the door praying he would find all well inside. He took out his gun as a precaution. He closed the door and locked as well as latched it. He made his way into the bedroom along the wall.

"John, is that you?" she asked. "Speak now because I've got you covered. One false move and you're a dead man."

"Yes, Sue, it's me. I'm all right. Lower your weapon. I'm putting mine away now."

"Why did you come in locked and loaded?"

"It's been a long night. Can we go to sleep?"

"I couldn't sleep knowing you were out there somewhere."

"I'm here now. Relax. I'm going to grab a shower. I'm a mess. I've been hiding and crouching in sumac. If you get near me, you're likely to be contaminated."

"Poison sumac?"

"Is there any other kind?"

She turned on the light. He saw her concerned look and her pistol hanging down in her right hand. Fulghum knew he must look awful. He waved her back to bed and went to the bathroom where he stripped off his clothes. He ran the shower until the temperature felt right. Then he stepped into the stall and soaped himself. He was careful not to scrub too hard lest the broken glass cut him. When he had rinsed himself, he stepped out of the shower.

She stood there waiting for him with a large towel. She wrapped it around his shoulders and helped him dry off.

"Come to bed. I can see you need to sleep. If you want to tell me about it when we wake up, that's fine."

"Sue, I'm glad you stayed right here. I ran into trouble, but things turned out all right."

"Was it something like what happened this morning?"

"As a matter of fact, yes, it was. I was lucky again to have a friend along. You won't believe what happened to my car. The windshield was blown out with glass everywhere inside. Bullet holes make the exterior look like a Buick four-hole model. I picked up your car on the way back and deposited what was left of mine in the long-term parking lot."

"Mine will get us to Pittsfield. Don't worry."

"I won't stop worrying until we get to the bottom of this mystery and sort out who's doing this to us. Let's get some sleep. What time did you set the alarm for our wake up?"

"Seven o'clock."

"Perfect. I'll just have a couple of fingers of JD to help me sleep."

"Mind if I join you? I'll pour two." She rose to pour more Jack Daniels whiskey in two glasses.

"Thanks. One thing bothers me." His brow furrowed and he shook his head.

"What's that, John?"

"How the hell did the snipers know to set up where they did? I didn't know where I was going until my friend told me where we were going."

"Doesn't that tell you something?" she asked, innocently.

"I don't want to go there, Sue." Fulghum thought Agency involvement in the attempted assassination was highly likely, but he was unsure how it worked. Was the Agency trying to assassinate him by proxy using DPRK assets? Was a rogue element within the CIA, sympathetic to the DPRK, trying to keep a black program from becoming visible? If either of those questions could be answered in the affirmative, then Ken Mander was also in the cross hairs. Perhaps it was better not to "over think" the problem. Intelligence matters often remained blurry at best.

"I'm sorry, John, but you are there already. And I am also." She smiled ruefully and handed him a glass, taking a moment to touch hers to it. "Drink your JD. Maybe things will be clearer in the morning."

"Gunbae," he toasted.

"Gunbae, and good night."

They both downed their whiskeys then Fulghum fell into bed. She covered him and slid in beside him, pressing her body next to his. His arm wrapped over her head on her pillow. She kissed him but got no response. She knew he was fast asleep. This made her smile. She breathed easily now that he was back and safe. Then she fell asleep and did not awaken until the alarm sounded in the morning.

While Sue prepared for their meeting, Fulghum answered Pounce's call on his cell phone.

"Hi Nigel, what's up?"

"I thought you'd like to know I'm interviewing a woman named Cecily Portius. She's the Judge's vulpine sister's great granddaughter. She has, she admits, always hated her great grand uncle for what he put her great grandmother through. Her great grandmother's husband died a horrible death and left nothing to support her. The Judge took his sister into his home and allowed her to raise her great-granddaughter Cecily there. Cecily was a rival to Freddie for the Judge's largesse, but the Judge was a stingy man. Now Cecily is staying under the Judge's roof because she's in an advanced stage of pregnancy but has no husband. She told me she has nowhere else to go."

"All right, Nigel. Why is she of particular interest in your case?"

"On many occasions, she's told others she wished the Judge were dead. She understood she was to inherit a large amount of money upon his death. Her Korean maid has just conveyed the news to me that Cecily had gone into premature labor. A physician was summoned quickly, yet the unborn child died, followed shortly afterward by the death of her mother."

"So you've lost another suspect?"

"That's right. But there's more - Riley and Shaunessy have been digging. Other inquiries I initiated have begun to bear fruit. Were you aware Anderson's brothers and sisters have all died recently, together with many of their children?"

"Have you made a list?"

"It'll be in your inbox in minutes. When are you going to arrive here? It's high time we went night fishing again."

"I expect to leave Boston around noon. I can meet you pier side as before at ten thirty unless I call to wave you off first."

"You can't come too soon. How have things been on that end?"

"Compared with what you've been going through, my problems are minor."

"I won't believe that. Anyway, I've got to get back to the grindstone. No rest for the weary. Later." Pounce terminated the call.

"Sue, did you overhear that?"

"No. I had my hair blower on full power. What's happened?" She came out of the bathroom making her hair up into a pile with the two hair sticks artfully planted to keep her coils sitting just right. Fulghum was impressed. She looked stunning, and her eyes sparkled.

"Cecily Portius and her premature newborn have just died of suspected poisoning."

"The greedy bitch! She deserved worse. I'm glad she's gone. The loss of the innocent baby is a shame."

" Cecily's death is another in a long line. I've just learned about the deaths of all Anderson's brothers and sisters and most of their children."

"That's old news. They've been dying like flies. Aging does that, don't you know?"

"I wonder how many of those deaths were from old age and how many were induced by poison."

Fulghum's cell phone rang. Caller ID showed Silvia as the caller. With a finger to his lips, Fulghum signaled Sue to be quiet as he answered the phone.

"Good morning, Silvia."

"Hello, John. We've just received news of a shootout outside the AMTRAK University Avenue stop. That's near enough our rendezvous to be suspicious. I thought you should know as we converge on Mr. Ives."

"Thanks, Silvia. It's probably a drug deal that went horribly wrong. The new heroin traffic will bring that kind of activity."

"Well, be careful on your way. I'll see you there. Ciao."

Sue pursed her lips and squinted at Fulghum. "You were involved in the shootout, weren't you? It had nothing to do with the drug traffic."

"Are you ready to leave yet?"

"I'll just freshen up my makeup. It won't take long."

"You look terrific right now." He admired her while she did a pirouette. She bowed slightly.

"Thank you, but you men don't realize how hard it is to look beautiful. The slightest blemish can spoil the whole effect. I like the natural look. That's harder to create than the usual cosmetics, especially when you have my skin tone. The man we are going to visit is going to have five to ten seconds to form an impression. We want him to respond positively and talk, don't we? I thought so. I'll just be one minute more. Did you clean your gun this morning?"

"Yes. I did that before you awakened. Force of habit. Military training. Anyway, it's cleaned, oiled, fully loaded and safed."

"So's mine. I worked on it while I was waiting for you to return last night. There, I'm done now. How do I look?" She walked right up to him and looked him in the eyes. He smiled, held her at arm's length and asked her to turn around.

"Perfect! I'll load the baggage into the car. Check one last time to be sure we haven't forgotten anything. We won't be coming back. Check out is automatic."

He put his card key on the table and grabbed the luggage. Sue put on her dark glasses and followed Fulghum out the door. They loaded the luggage into the trunk, and Fulghum drove. In ten minutes, they parked outside the home where Clancy Frew, aka Mr. Ives, resided. As they got out of the car, Silvia pulled up and joined them. Silvia was dressed in a robin's egg blue dress. She had tied a matching ribbon in her hair. Her outfit was in stark contrast to the black business outfit which Sue wore in her role as Fulghum's assistant.

Silvia kissed John on the cheek in greeting and turned towards Sue with a proprietary look in her eye.

"Silvia, this is Kim Su Baek, also known as Sue. She's my executive assistant."

Silvia raised her eyebrows and scanned the slender Korean wearing the dark glasses. She extended her hand, and Sue shook it firmly.

Silvia turned back to John. "We're going to be right on time, John. Since I set up the meeting, I'll take the lead."

"Lead on, Silvia. Thank you again for arranging this meeting. It's likely to be critical."

Silvia signed in for the three at the desk. An orderly who was standing by ushered them back to a private room where Clancy was seated in a wheelchair looking out the floor-to-ceiling glass onto an immaculate garden.

The orderly announced them, and Clancy maneuvered his wheelchair so he could see his guests.

Silvia extended her hand. "Mr. Clancy, my name is Silvia Blackwood." He shook her hand and looked towards Fulghum. "This is Mr. John Fulghum and his assistant Kim Su Baek." He shook Fulghum's extended hand then he moved his hand towards Sue. She took off her shades with her left hand and moved close, extending her right hand. Something in the way she did this brought Clancy fully alert yet mesmerized by the young woman's eyes.

"I'm very pleased to meet you, Mr. Clancy." The man took her hand and held it gently.

"Remarkable," he said. "Please sit down so we can talk."

"What's remarkable?" Fulghum asked him.

"Her eyes are her father's eyes down to the sparkle."

"What do you mean by her father's eyes, Mr. Clancy?" asked Silvia, intrigued.

"This young woman has the same green-flecked brown eyes which Major Anderson had. I'd never seen eyes like those before. I haven't seen any since then. My dear," he asked, "are you Anderson's daughter, or have I just made an old fool out of myself? It wouldn't be the first time." By the way, he said this Fulghum knew the man was no fool. His memory was sharp. His ability to integrate data was astounding.

"Yes, Mr. Clancy. Judge Anderson was my father."

"Please accept my deepest condolences on your loss."

She took out a handkerchief and dried her eyes. "Thank you."

"Mr. Clancy, her deceased father is the reason we're here today. The man was murdered. We're trying to help in the investigation of that murder. We think you can help us." Silvia then looked at Fulghum.

"Mr. Clancy, you once did investigative work in Korea leading to a major story about Stephen Anderson."

"Yes. The story might have won my associate and me the Pulitzer Prize, but it was spiked. Our notes were seized and put in some damn archive. We were paid a large bonus and told never to investigate further or publish any of the material. We were also told a bulletin interdicting any such material had been sent to every major news outlet in the country. That effectively ended our journalistic careers. I turned to writing potboilers under a pseudonym. My associate and friend became a ghostwriter for the rich and famous. He died five or so years ago."

Silvia said, "We'd like to revisit the last interview you had with Anderson. We aren't looking to publish what you tell us. We only want to know the substance. Mr. Fulghum does have a few particular questions to ask, but we'd like you to sit back and tell us what you remember."

Clancy looked at Sue and shook his head. "I suppose a daughter has a right to know a few things about her father that don't appear in print. Of course, it was a long time ago. I don't remember everything. Have you seen the notes in the archive?"

Silvia looked at Fulghum. "Mr. Clancy, we'd like to hear your story straight from you. Your memories will be pure gold. All the rest is dross."

"Call the orderly and get us lemonades with a bowl of sliced limes. Talking makes me thirsty."

Sue rose and arranged for the drinks. Meanwhile, Clancy meditated on the particulars of his story. When the drinks arrived, Clancy proposed a toast to Anderson's memory.

"Gunbae," he said and drained his glass dry. The others followed suit. Sue poured another round of lemonade. With his eyes fixed on Sue, Clancy began his tale. It was clear to John and Silvia his entire focus was to make the event vivid for the surviving daughter and not for them. For her part, Sue leaned forward wide-eyed to catch every word.

Clancy gave the background for the interview with the heroic major, who then lay convalescing in a special military hospital in Seoul. Two Korean women, a mother and her daughter, were watching over him. The major was lucid in his thinking and deeply appreciative of his caretakers. He had been through hell, but he had more on his mind than his successful mission.

"That's where we knew we had a story. Everything that had been put out about his mission was so much malarkey spun out as whole cloth to cover up the truth. But we wanted the true story, and we got it."

Clancy continued to recount the story as Anderson had told it - the details of the mission, the shoot down and the rendezvous with South Korean intelligence agents behind enemy lines. How they learned of the Soviet advisor and his location, the self-appointed mission to apprehend him, the fighting return to the American front lines, then the transport to the UN intelligence people. Finally, the struggle, that resulted in the Congressional Medal of Honor on the one hand and a pledge of eternal silence on the other.

"That's, of course, when the trouble began. Perhaps we need more lemonade. I need a rest break. Maybe you do too."

While Sue arranged for more lemonade and cookies, everyone took a moment to stretch their legs. When the food arrived, Sue excused herself to freshen up. Clancy resumed his story only when she returned.

"You mentioned trouble when we left off," Fulghum said. Clancy's eyes went back to Sue and stayed there while he continued.

"Yes. The Soviet agent's kidnapping caught everyone off balance. No one wanted to admit the depth of the Russian involvement in the Korean War. We had the smoking gun of their sponsorship of biological weapons in the theater. The high command wanted the issue to just go away, but they couldn't kill the man. Instead, they negotiated a trade behind the scenes. This caused consternation in the agents who had risked their lives to capture the Soviet clandestine operator and in Anderson, who was livid about the way American support for Korea was being managed. He railed about the lies and subterfuge. He said all the negotiations about peace would end without a treaty. Fancy that, my dear. Your father was right."

Fulghum pulled a small folded paper from his pocket. "I wonder whether you remember the names O Sun Ma, Ri Bo An and Mu Un Li."

"I remember them vividly. They were the three men who were sitting in the room where we held the interview. I thought they must be Korean intelligence agents. They had the look. The two Korean nurses were there too. They stood behind Major Anderson the whole time, silently watching for their moment to do service. No one else was in that room. The

Americans let us alone. I suppose that's why they confiscated our notes when we were done."

"So the military confiscated your notes?"

"No. Nothing of the kind. Our press representative in country came to demand the notes. He said he was in a jam. He said our notes had to be censored before publication. That was a lie. There would be no publication. I later discovered when I tried to get the notes back that they were in the possession of our employer, the Boston Globe. Of course, the Globe denied it. A little bird told me those notes were in the archives, but I could never find a way to get them. They're probably still in the archives today. I don't know, and I don't care anymore."

The four mused on what Clancy had said.

"Mr. Clancy, did you have the impression at the time of your interview that Major Anderson had a special relationship with the South Korean cause?"

"Definitely. He was the only American soldier I met who was fluent in Hangul. Those three Korean intelligence agents were the same men who kept him safe and helped him capture the Soviet operator."

Silvia asked, "While you were in Korea, were you warned against publication by the Koreans themselves?"

"It's funny you should mention it. The US government made me sign papers attesting I wouldn't publish anything relating to Anderson for fifty years. The Korean government was even more demanding. They made me sign papers extending that time frame to life. So technically, I still can't publish by Korean rules of the game. Our government visited me once every ten years for a checkup. The Koreans never visited after that first time."

"Did you or your associate ever attempt to visit Anderson after you saw him in Korea?"

"No. We went on to do other things. Not publishing our piece on Anderson stuck in my craw. I've never gotten over it."

"This is a long shot, Mr. Clancy, but do you have any idea who might have murdered Anderson? The man was just over one hundred years old." Fulghum sat forward watching Clancy closely for his reaction to the question.

"If I were writing one of my pulp novels, I'd make it a government operation, tying up loose ends of ancient history to protect current operations with legacy roots."

"Humor me with how the plot might work."

"All right. This is impromptu, but it might work. Let's say Anderson worked on black projects for the South Korean government after the Armistice was signed. After all, the Korean War has never ended. His involvement would have been embarrassing to our government, but what could they do about it? Hell, he was a bona fide war hero. If he was sharp until the end, he could have continued his work. He might even have operations running now though he is dead. Anyway, at some point he and all his history have to be erased. A government would take time to set up such an operation. In execution, it would have to be immediate and comprehensive."

"So when Anderson was eliminated, everyone touching him or any documentation pointing to what he did would have to be eliminated too."

"That's right, but you know, governments can't be all seeing and all knowing though they'd like to be. What do you think?"

"Mr. Clancy, I think we've taken up far too much of your time. Out of curiosity, are you now working on a new book?"

"I've always got a new book going. I also have a couple of ideas for others. Maybe today I've been given an idea. Who knows? Anyway, thanks for stopping by to see me especially you, my dear. Again, I'm very sorry for your loss. Your father was a great man before and after I met him. It was a great privilege to know him. Goodbye."

When they left the private room, Clancy wheeled himself around to look out the glass window at the garden. Out front in the parking lot, the three gathered for a moment to recap what had just happened.

"Thank you again, Silvia, for arranging the meeting. I've confirmed what I learned from the papers from the archive. I've also gotten a couple of new ideas."

"Let's hope Mr. Clancy lives to a ripe old age and dies of natural causes."

"Does anyone die of natural causes anymore?" Sue asked.

John and Silvia looked at Sue with astonishment. "So young and so cynical?" Silvia asked.

"The Roman satirist Juvenal posed the same question two thousand years ago. Well, Silvia, we're going to drive out to Pittsfield. I'll be available on my cell."

She moved in quickly and kissed him on the lips. "Be careful, John." She looked daggers at Sue. "You take care of him, or you'll answer to me."

"Yes, ma'am. Are you ready, John?"

"We're outta here."

While John and Sue buckled up, Silvia drove out of the facility, headed back to her Globe office. Sue reached behind Fulghum's seat, pulled out a CD and popped it in the player under the radio. Recordings of wind chimes began.

"These tones are comforting. Relax and don't worry; I got everything Clancy said on tape so we can review it whenever you're ready. It's going to be a long day's drive."

"Fortunately, I transferred my fishing gear from my car to yours at the long term lot."

"Fishing gear?"

"I thought I'd do some late night fishing when we get to Pittsfield. Did you know that long ago someone took a four-foot pike out of Onota Lake?"

"I hate fishing."

"Maybe you don't have the right approach."

"It's the slime and scales I don't like."

"Catch and release is my motto."

"I don't want that to apply to my father's murderer, John. The release part, I mean. When Mr. Clancy hinted that a government might have been behind my father's murder, did you believe him?"

"Stranger things have happened, Sue. Say, I like this recording of wind chimes. Let's enjoy our ride. The exit for the Mass Pike is coming right up. There's not a cloud in the sky."

Chapter 7

The Grand Assembly

Fulghum made sure Sue was situated in a comfortable suite at the Hotel on North in Pittsfield. They planned that the suite would be their command center for observing what was happening at the estate. The amenities at the Berkshire resort would keep Sue occupied, he thought. Fulghum rendezvoused with Pounce for his fishing date at ten thirty. As before, they motored well out on the lake before they began to discuss the latest events in the Anderson case.

"Tomorrow I've ordered the assembly of all players in the Judge's study at the estate. I hope you and Miss Kim will join us for the occasion."

"Who else is coming?"

"Let's see. The Police Commissioner, Anderson's lawyer's partner, Anderson's trust officer, a handwriting expert, Anderson's physician and all the remaining household including the downstairs maid and the butler."

"It sounds as if you're aiming to do the magic of a mystery novel. Let me guess. You're going to unmask the murderer in public in such a way that you get an instant confession."

"Don't mock me, John. We're only going to review the case in such a way that everyone will understand what the others have been deposing."

"Do you think the murderer will be in the room?"

"I certainly hope so. I also hope we don't have any more corpses."

"Somehow, I don't think the omelet is going to unscramble itself."

"Okay. Give me your current assessment as an outsider. Sometimes being right in the middle clouds the perspective. I talked with Molly earlier today. She told me to listen to what you have to say. So I'm all ears."

Fulghum lit a cigarette and looked out on the black water.

"I'm convinced we're looking at a government operation. The question is which government is involved?"

"Please explain that."

"No fewer than five governments had a reason to keep what Anderson knew under wraps. The United States, South Korea, North Korea, the Peoples Republic of China and the Russian Federation. I won't bore you with how China and Russia may play since either or both may have worked with North Korea."

"Okay, that leaves America, South Korea, and the DPRK. What do you think?"

"We censored the interviews of the two reporters who interviewed Anderson after his heroic run into North Korea during the hostile phase of the Korean War. South Korea also censored the interviews. Yet records of Anderson's exploits remain."

"Do you mean the notebooks in the Korean language?"

"Yes, and notes made by the two reporters during the interview done in the Fifties."

"Do those notes still exist?"

"Between us, yes. For anyone else's consumption, no. This morning I conferred with the only surviving witness to the interview with Anderson verifying the truth of the documents I read before burning them."

"I'll assume you had a good reason for burning what might have been evidence in a murder trial. "

Fulghum nodded.

"All right. What did you learn from those documents?"

"Anderson was working for the KCIA from the time just after his plane crashed behind enemy lines in North Korea until the day he was murdered."

"Jesus."

"Yeah. It gets lots better, but the short version is that he was at the center of a South Korean operation against North Korea in CONUS."

"Are you shitting me?"

"Friend, I shit you not. Anderson's Korean nurses and EAs were his assassins. He targeted North Korean clandestine operatives who were sent to the US to assassinate major figures or commit sabotage against strategic targets. That's what the notebooks document in minute detail all the way back to the Armistice through today. The key to deciphering the notebooks is now residing in the finest five-star hotel in the Berkshires."

"Kim Su Baek?"

"I call her Sue."

"So what are you two up to? Give me the censored version, please."

"We're scrutinizing one of the notebooks while we continue to appraise all the characters you're assessing through your interviews. She knows all those people well. She can give details about them you won't be able to elicit in your interviews."

"I'll want to include the notebook in my evidence pile."

"We can make that happen if this ever goes to trial."

"Given the possible government involvement, this case may not go to trial."

"I think we should proceed on the basis that the government involvement doesn't exist."

"Why?"

"Someone must be operating on a government's behalf. That doesn't preclude our following the evidence where it leads and prosecuting with what we know. I believe we can identify the murderer. That person may or may not be aware he or she is acting as an agent of a government. In any case, a murderer is still a murderer in the eyes of the law."

Pounce sat musing on this thought for a long while. His line extended well back of the trolling motorboat. His Rapala lure was ten to twelve feet below the surface, tugging slightly against his partially bowed fishing rod. Fulghum smoked while he thought.

"John, I understand things have gotten pretty hot for you. I'll bet you're sorry you got mixed up in this case."

"I had no idea I was going to open a stinking can of worms when the girl walked through my office door. I should have known better."

"You barely survived one three-man hit team in your own apartment."

"I survived because Sue was a good shot and I was lucky."

"You don't mean it?"

"She's KCIA, Nigel. One of their best. She was trusted to take care of her father because she was his daughter. When she walked into my office, she had just lost both her mother and her father. She was guided by her father's instructions, passed through her father's lawyer, who is now also dead. A gutsy girl."

"And beautiful."

"No argument there. She has her father's eyes. That's what the reporter said this morning. It's why he opened up and told us his story."

"It's a tragic business."

"Nigel, there was a second three-man hit team."

"University Avenue station?"

"Yes. If Ken Mander hadn't been with me that night, I'd not be here fishing with you."

"So you survived two attempts on your life by separate three-man hit teams?"

"That's right. I've learned recently that Korean hit teams are deployed in threes."

"How do you know?"

"The original team which worked with Anderson in Korea was comprised of three men."

"Are you thinking KCIA is the common denominator?"

"Not exactly. I believe DPRK operations are run as a mirror of KCIA. Our CIA thinks the two hit teams were sent by North Korea. A North Korean three-person team was also sent against you and failed."

"That's news to me."

"You had no need to know. What I'm having trouble processing is why the DPRK would be intent on eliminating you and me. My hypothesis is that we each have part of a puzzle. When we put the pieces together, we'll know the answer."

"I hope you're right."

"While Sue and I drove out here, the topic of Anderson's aversion to doctors and traditional medicines came up. She thought one reason for his longevity was his insistence on eating nothing but healthy foods, vitamins, and minerals."

"That seems to have worked for him."

"Perhaps it would have kept on working except for the arsenic poisoning. Who knows how long the man might have lived. The validated human record is something over 126 years."

"I suppose Sue told you the secret of eternal life?"

"Something like that. Anderson had annual high colonics with pure grass juice to cleanse his system. Sue gave him a vitamin and mineral regimen twice a day. He took the pills with coconut milk. He mostly ate raw greens, so much so that the staff called him 'the rabbit' behind his back. He bathed in one of those stand-up bathtubs and scrubbed his whole body with a loofa sponge."

"Spare me the details, John."

"I only want to make a point. We're going to have to discover who gave him the vitamin and mineral mix once Sue had left to take care of her mother. She claims no one but her mother and she could get the right combination of pills. Can you read my mind?"

"You think that whoever gave Anderson his pills might have given him something else—like poison—as well?"

"That could be so, but it wouldn't necessarily account for what killed Sue's mother. Sue is checking out another angle."

"What's that?

"Do you know anything about chelates?"

"This sounds like the prelude to one of those Jeopardy! questions."

"Chelates bind with harmful heavy metals such as arsenic and carry them out of the body."

"Maybe Anderson didn't take enough chelates?"

"That could be, or perhaps he never took chelates until very recently. Sue told me he and her mother had just received a box of PectaSol® tablets, which are advertised to remove arsenic, specifically, like nothing else available."

"Okay, so he and his wife may have taken this supplement. So what?"

"This is going to take a little explaining. So hang on. What if Anderson never took chelates before he took the PectaSol®. Let's further say he always ate a lot of rice and other veggies with high arsenic content. That makes sense because he was surrounded by Koreans who did his cooking. Sue told me he had so much arsenic in his system that if he suddenly started taking PectaSol®, he'd likely get symptoms of arsenic poisoning because it was being concentrated as the substance ran through his body."

"So the antidote might have become the poison?"

"It's just her theory at this point. If it were the case, we might have an instance where PectaSol® became the vehicle for the killing agent arsenic."

"That's a little lame. Besides, it wouldn't account for the lawyer's death, would it?"

"It certainly wouldn't account for the three hit teams. Hold on a minute." He looked at his cell phone and said, "I'm getting a call from Silvia."

Pounce shrugged.

Fulghum answered the call. "Hi, Silvia. What's up?"

"Where are you right now?"

"I'm sitting in a motorboat trolling on Lake Onota in Pittsfield, Massachusetts."

"I thought you might like to know that the person we visited today has just died."

"Oh hell. How did you find out?"

"The police called from the care facility to ask whether we witnessed any symptoms in Clancy that might indicate a poisoning."

"So they think he was poisoned?"

"They won't know for certain until the lab work is completed, but that's their current theory."

"I guess we were unlucky for him."

"You know what I'm thinking."

"You think Sue had something to do with the man's death. I'll have to think about it. Are you all right?"

"I'm fine. I just want you to be very careful you aren't harboring a viper in your nest."

"Thanks for the heads up. If you can't reach me on my cell, leave a voicemail message. You know our prearranged emergency signal. Don't hesitate to use it if necessary."

"John, I also got a call from Darcy Figlear around an hour after we left Clancy."

"Why did she call?"

"She called to warn me about the consequences of our visiting Clancy."

"Was she specific about the nature of the threat?"

"No. She just said to watch my back. I'm doing that."

"Good. Try to get a good night's sleep if you can manage it. I'm going into the lions' den tomorrow morning."

"Be careful John. Good night." She terminated the call before he could respond.

"So another man has died for the cause. The KIA count is rising by the day. Are you going to pull this murder into your investigation?"

"I won't do that unless I'm ordered to do it. Having just overheard your conversation, I'd say Silvia, Sue and you have reason to be vigilant."

"The same goes for you, my friend. Let's leave nothing to chance."

"As for your strategy tomorrow, be confident and watch out for unintended consequences."

The fishermen decided to return to the pier. Pounce leapt to the pier while Fulghum kept trolling. Around a hundred yards along the shore, Fulghum reeled in and made up the two lines. He turned in the motorboat and the equipment at the boathouse. Then he drove back to his hotel where he found Sue playing Angry Birds on her laptop computer.

"Any luck fishing?" she asked.

"The fish had all the luck tonight. The only bites were mosquito bites. Where did you hide the JD? We've got to be at the estate tomorrow morning to participate in a big meeting in your father's study. Everyone will be present, except for the deceased."

"I'll find a bottle and pour two. You can tell me what's happening while I do it."

"Clancy's dead."

"What? Oh, no!" She turned white as a sheet and had a hard time keeping her balance as she walked. "Now I know we need some whiskey. Who told you about it?"

"Silvia called."

"How did she know?"

"The police called her. As you may recall, she signed the visitors' log when we entered the home."

"Are they sure Clancy died by poison?"

"Forensic analysis is now being performed. We'll know by this afternoon."

"We seem to be bad luck for everyone we meet."

"Sue, did you have anything to do with Clancy's death?"

"How can you say such a thing?"

"You were alone with the lemonade and cookies while everyone else was making a pit stop. Silvia certainly didn't kill him. I'm also innocent."

"You really think I killed him, the one person who could verify my father's role since Korea? If I am the killer, why haven't I killed you?"

"Probably because I'm your Prince Charming."

"Look, it's four o'clock in the morning. I'm going to have some JD. You can have some too if you aren't afraid I spiked it with sayak. What time did you say we have to arrive at the estate?"

"I didn't state a time. We should be there by nine o'clock. The police are providing English breakfast."

"Will there be a taster present?" Sue asked this with a grim smile.

"What did you say? Please say it again. It's important."

"I said, 'Will there be a taster present?'"

"Now that's the best idea of the new day. Let's have our whiskey and hit the hay."

They had two fingers of Jack Daniels and lay beside each other with their separate thoughts. He was in his underwear while she was dressed in her gold silk robe. Silently, Fulghum set the alarm for seven o'clock and chastely kissed Sue goodnight. Then they rolled aside and slept until daylight.

When they arrived at the main gate, two Pittsfield policemen were standing guard and eating donuts. They checked Fulghum's and Kim's identification against names on a clipboard and waved them through to park in the graveled area in front of the entrance. Like an executive and his assistant, they went to the door and knocked. The butler opened the door with a surprised look to see Miss Kim with a strange man. Fulghum handed over his business card. The butler told him to come into the vestibule and wait while he conferred with the authorities.

Officer Riley came to escort them into the enormous room styled as the Judge's study. Ranged around the walls were wild game trophies, including the heads of a black rhinoceros, a lion, an African elephant and a kudu. Japanese suits of armor stood like ghost sentinels in all four corners of the room. On the floor was a massive Chinese rug.

The downstairs maid offered Fulghum and Sue ginseng tea with a curtsy. Sue asked that hers be served with milk. Fulghum wanted his with a lemon. When the tea came, Riley interdicted and took the full teacups away before they could be tasted. He roughly escorted the pair to seats against the wall at the back of the room.

Frowning, Riley whispered, "You're to sit here. Don't eat or drink anything, no matter who serves it to you. Officer Pounce demands this."

The officer returned to his duty as the primary receptionist for the guests. Each guest had been assigned a specific spot in a range of seats facing a dais with the Judge's desk and chair at its center.

While the other guests arrived, Sue told Fulghum the histories of all the artifacts in the room, including the glass-encased library volumes, among them a Shakespeare First Folio and the originals of all the plays of Beaumont and Fletcher. Sue proudly announced her father had collected the complete extant works of the classical Korean sijo poets and hyangga songwriters. She told him the story behind the novel The Poet, by Yi Munyol.

"Cultivated Koreans," she said, "had to pass Chinese written examinations to be admitted to the civil service, just as Chinese did in China. Before the annexation of Korea by Japan, the Joseon kingdom set the rules. That was the era of sayak. The so-called modernization followed in 1910. Those pots around the floor by the walls are all Joseon pots. You'll have to examine them carefully. They're beautiful and priceless."

Sue was about to launch into a history of Korea from the beginning of the Joseon period in 1392 forward when Fulghum hushed her so they could observe the other participants in Pounce's séance.

Behind the desk where Pounce would sit, stood Officers Riley and Shaunessy on either side, like sentinels with their hands behind them and their feet close together. The Police Commissioner sat in the front rank of seats. The surviving Anderson family members sat in the same row and the row behind. The next row behind those included the handwriting expert. It also included the butler, Albert Maynard and his wife, Sadie. Next to them sat the gardener, Bi Wan Bo and his wife, Taitai. Miss Lin, the housemaid, was next in line then sat the infamous prostitute Madame Ko and a burly man who appeared to be the Madame's Korean bodyguard. Also seated in the room were the deceased family lawyer's law partner and a collection of men and women who remained unidentified.

Without ceremony, Pounce entered when all the guests were present. He opened his proceedings stating dramatically, "The murderer of Judge Anderson and his wife is in this room."

The guests repositioned themselves on their chairs and leaned forward to hear what he had to say.

"Can everyone hear me, or do I need to raise my voice?"

Fulghum nodded indicating he could hear even though he was seated at the back wall. Pounce nodded back and continued.

"Very well. If everyone will remain quiet, I think we'll manage. Recently-made discoveries and unfortunate deaths narrow the field of suspects considerably."

He paused and reached for his teacup, but instead of drinking the tea the housemaid had served him, he motioned for Officer Shaunessy to pick it up. The man did so and left the room.

Unbeknownst to the assemblage, the officer left the estate to deliver Pounce's cup with its contents along with the cups earlier served to Fulghum and Sue to a local chemist for rapid analysis.

Pounce droned on, sifting through the steps he had taken in his investigation and repeating the accounts contained in each signed deposition. He read the documents slowly and deliberately, raising his head from time to time to be sure his audience was listening. He saw the Commissioner yawn more than once during the forty-five-minute declaration.

Finally, Pounce looked up from his papers and announced, "I've discovered that despite the many twists and turns of his family relations, there is another legitimate child who is not acknowledged in the family. Anderson's recently deceased former executive assistant was not only his secret love child but also his fourth wife. She gave birth to Kim Su Baek, his last executive assistant."

Pounce paused for effect while the assemblage murmured and looked back at Miss Kim with keen interest.

He glared at his audience and waited for them to become quiet. Then he continued, "I've also learned the Judge had a practice of loaning his executive assistants and others from his intimate household to other relatives from time to time. In fact, he did so whenever he wanted to alter the family's inheritance arrangements. We conclude from an examination of all the formal documents that the Judge realigned his will, trusts and life insurance policies regularly, so they reflected changes in the composition of his family as well as his personal whims."

Again, Pounce paused for effect. He then seemed to be preoccupied. He shuffled through some papers he had laid on the desk as if looking for something. He drew out a piece of paper and scanned it with his eyes.

"For example, the Judge's elder brother and his wife died under mysterious circumstances two years ago. Summarily they and their heirs were all stricken from his will and trusts. His younger sister also died unaccountably just months before both parents of the Judge went on a sea voyage from which they didn't return alive. Notably, the Judge's Korean executive assistant, mother of Kim Su Baek, had gone with his parents on the voyage."

Pounce now had the participants spellbound. Occasionally the audience looked around to gauge the others' reactions to what they were hearing.

"While the huge corpus of the Judge's parents' estates was still being held in escrow pending probate of their wills, Anderson's immediate relatives and all their heirs were immediately stricken from his own will and trusts.

"I hesitate to draw the logical conclusions. The matter is complex. The ways of an established, wealthy family are sometimes inscrutable to outsiders, particularly when the lawyer who created the documents in question was suddenly murdered before he could be consulted. Under the circumstances, I have to wonder whether the eldest son's copy of the last will and testament of the Judge is the correct one. In fact, another, presumably final version of the Judge's will is in the possession of Kim Su Baek. This version, postdating the last his eldest son was aware of, leaves the entire estate to Kim

Su Baek in the event of the simultaneous deaths of the Judge and his wife."

The assemblage gasped in a single admission of stupefaction at this news. The Commissioner showed signs of new life as he sat up straight in his chair and appeared to be straining to hear every word Pounce was saying.

"Unlike prior versions, this final will leaves nothing whatsoever to the butler and his wife or the gardener and his wife. The handwriting expert, who is seated in the third row here, has attested under oath that the Judge's signature on the will is genuine. He has also validated the signatures of the will's two witnesses. I won't call him forward, but if he will raise his hand now if what I have said is correct, that will suffice."

The handwriting expert raised his hand and waved. Pounce then moved to his next subject.

"I remind you all that 'simultaneous death' is defined within the will as 'within the space of seventy-two hours.' The decedent and the decedent's wife died within that interval. The coroner, who is present, can attest to that. Again, in the interest of time, please raise your hand to indicate what I've said is correct."

The coroner raised his hand and held it in the air for a moment before lowering it.

The butler and gardener arose in protest, the latter shouting. "Everything you've just said points to the guilt of Kim Su Baek, as the murderer, or rather murderess."

A great hubbub arose in the room. People began to shout their agreement until Pounce looked at Officer Riley. The enormous and imposing officer stepped forward menacingly and put his hand on his pistol, which remained strapped into its holster. Everyone who was standing and muttering sat, calmed down, and became quiet again. Riley went back to his position behind the desk. Pounce proceeded with his statement.

"The executive assistant's copy of the will does raise a conundrum. Yes, it gives her a motive for murder because of the inheritance terms, but it also gives every Anderson family member as well as the butler and the gardener motives as well because they were all effectively disinherited by it."

Now the family members, the butler, and the gardener looked at their feet in confusion.

"I ask emphatically, who is the murderer? The family members were convinced that the copy of the will known to the eldest son Harry was the definitive document. They had no idea another will had been created to supersede it. The butler and the gardener seem too surprised by the news to have been aware the change to the will was made. Their lack of awareness makes their motives disappear. Besides, everyone knows about Madame Ko."

This time when Pounce paused, everyone laughed, including the butler.

"By your amusement, I guess you think you know about Madame Ko. But I don't think you know everything about her. I single out and mention Madame Ko because she has a special place in the pantheon of suspects who are gathered here today. We know of the peccadilloes—or worse—involving Mr. Maynard and her. What is not generally known is that Madame Ko's expertise goes far beyond running a house of ill repute. In fact, as most members of the Anderson family know, she's a talented money lender who has brokered loans against their imputed inheritance by nearly every member of the Anderson family. She is funded by one of the largest private lending organizations in this country - the collective women of the Korean-American community. I'm not speaking out of school, am I, Madame Ko, to suggest that you've arranged loans in the amount of hundreds of millions of dollars against the Anderson estate. I won't have you give the details now. I only want a confirmation that the loans exist. Please say the word, yes or no."

Madame Ko sat proudly in her chair and uttered, "Yes."

"I'm happy to say that Madame Ko has voluntarily told me she's willing to give me detailed accounts showing exactly how much Freddie Hill and Cecily Portius—may God rest their souls as well as the child of Cecily Portius—how very much they owed to Madame Ko's organization when they were murdered. Those murders are being investigated separately, and the huge loans are only part of the picture in those investigations. I raise the issue here because of the enormity of the aggregate loan value only informally mortgaged by this set of arrangements.

"I beg your indulgence for a moment while I recount the beneficial nature of the loan service Madame Ko provides. I'll be brief. The story of the death of Reverend O, formerly of the Democratic People's Republic of Korea will serve as an example. This reverend was disfavored by his flock because of his origin in the North Korea - a declared enemy of both South Korea and the United States. The women who financed his congregation decided to fire their reverend without providing any alternative means of living for him. When Reverend O was informed of this decision, he went to his vehicle and extracted his loaded handgun. He returned to the church meeting room where the women sat with their husbands and shot them all. He set fire to the church and then went back to the parking area. He climbed into his car and shot himself in the mouth. The church burned to the ground. The corpses inside it were unrecognizable. As a result of this event, which caused the Korean community a tremendous loss of face, a great many families were placed in a difficult position.

Madame Ko entered the scene and provided the money to rebuild the church, provide money to all the families who had suffered losses and to hire a new reverend. If what I have said is not far from the truth, Madame Ko, please raise your hand."

Madame Ko and the Korean gentleman who sat beside her both raised their hands.

"Ladies and gentlemen, the ways of this informal network of beneficial loans is worldwide. It cuts across North and South Korea as well as the United States. Since the loans against the presumed heirs of Judge Anderson are more than equivalent to the corpus of the estate itself, an enormous problem is evident from Madame Ko's point of view when the collateral for those loans has been mortgaged not once over, but many times over in the course of the last sixty years."

"Then Madame Ko had the best motive for killing the Judge. It was revenge!" The gardener rose in a fury and shook his fist at Madame Ko. Her burly companion turned and worked his hands, deciding how to dismember his potential victim.

"Officer Riley, please restore order in this room."

Riley stood forward again and put his hand on his weapon. This time he unstrapped his pistol before he gripped its stock. The assemblage grew quiet. Now the entire Anderson family was caught between embarrassment at their loans having been discovered and anger at Madame Ko for putting them in the limelight through her discussions with Officer Pounce.

"Relax everyone. Madame Ko didn't murder Judge Anderson. As a matter of fact, she, among all of you, stood to gain most by the Judge's surviving. In fact, I can show you evidence she was the one who suggested the Judge use PectaSol® to bring his own and his wife's levels of arsenic and other toxic poisons down to a non-lethal level. Miss Kim, isn't it true that Madame Ko gave her sage advice to you and your mother some nine months ago, and you were excited about using the substance?"

Sue looked at Officer Pounce and then scanned the other faces that were suddenly trained on her.

"Yes. Madame Ko recommended organic, holistic vitamins and minerals as opposed to prescribed medicines. She also recommended high colonics with grass juice. We took her recommendations."

"And what was the efficacy of those measures?"

"Please clarify what you want me to say, Officer Pounce."

"When your father and mother took PectaSol®, how did it affect their health?"

"First let me say I administered the capsules morning and evening with their normal run of vitamins and minerals. In the initial four days after they started the regimen, both my father and my mother showed signs of arsenic poisoning."

"I thought the substance was supposed to eliminate arsenic from the system."

"Yes, but as it binds to the heavy metals in the system, it takes them through the normal channels of elimination. So anyone taking PectaSol® should accept such symptoms as signs of its effectiveness."

"After the initial signs, what happened?"

"My parents both recovered completely and presented better health and disposition."

"Miss Kim, please tell us what was your undergraduate major?"

"I did a double major in Analytical Chemistry and Human Anatomy."

"And what was the subject of your undergraduate thesis?"

"Synthesis of undetectable but lethal poisons."

Once again, the assemblage was in an uproar of accusations from all sides against Miss Kim. Pounce had to invoke Riley to restore order. The Police Commissioner himself now was taking an interest in Miss Kim. He raised his hand to ask a question.

Pounce nodded to the Commissioner.

"Officer Pounce, you have against Miss Kim prima facie evidence of a person who had the knowledge, the means, and the motive to kill Judge Anderson and his wife. What am I missing from this picture?"

"Commissioner, there is one critical thing missing from this picture. I'm expecting a clarification almost any minute. If everyone will be patient, all things will become clear. Miss Kim is a chemist by training and inclination. Perhaps the conclusive answer to the mystery lies in basic chemical analysis."

As if on cue, his cell phone rang. Pounce answered his phone and passed it to the Police Commissioner so he could hear for himself what the chemist had to say.

The Commissioner listened to the analytical chemist without speaking. Then he nodded and passed the phone back to Pounce as he sat back in his chair.

"Well, Commissioner. Please tell us what the chemist had to say."

"The sample cups, which contained the tea the housemaid served to Mr. John Fulghum and Miss Kim Su Baek, each contained tea with a lethal dose of arsenic poison."

The assemblage uttered another collective gasp.

The Commissioner waited until the room had quieted down. Then he continued, "Further, the cup of tea served to you, Officer Pounce, was similarly laced with a lethal dose of arsenic."

Pounce said, "For everyone's information, Officer Shaunessy delivered the cups in question to the chemist for analysis, and the chemist's analysis is now final."

"So, Officer Pounce, is the housemaid guilty of murder?" Riley blurted out.

"No, Officer Riley, it isn't quite that simple. The Korean tradition of sayak poisoning was a diabolical scheme. It was routinely used in public executions exactly as the Judge and his Korean employees employed it. Systematically, by means of arsenic poisoning, the Judge's relatives were eliminated. Then the Judge and his wife fell victim to it too."

"If the housemaid didn't perform the deed, who did?"

"Will the housemaid please stand?'

The poor woman stood, wringing her hands and weeping profusely.

"I had no idea the tea contained poison. I wouldn't kill a fly."

Pounce comforted her by saying, "I'm sure you wouldn't, Miss Lin. Will you, however, please tell us all who gave you the teacups to serve to the three people who've just been named?"

The woman trembled and looked around the room. With a wavering hand, she pointed at the butler but was too scared to speak.

The butler rose and pointed a gun at Officer Pounce.

"Enough of this nonsense!"

Pounce did not flinch, but simultaneously Riley, Fulghum, and Kim pulled their weapons and trained them on the butler. They were much too late.

The butler turned the barrel of his gun into his mouth to pull the trigger. A shot rang out, and the butler fell to the floor. People scattered to either side of the study. The Commissioner stood and kicked the gun out of the butler's hand. He gestured for Riley to pick the gun up with a cloth so as not to contaminate the evidence. Fulghum raced over and felt the butler's neck for a pulse but found none. He looked at Pounce and shook his head. Riley holstered his weapon and did as the Commissioner had directed. Sue holstered her weapon too and sat down watching everyone for signs of any other threat.

Pounce announced, "We've identified our murderer, and he has destroyed himself. Officer Riley, please dial 911."

Fulghum looked at Sue. She looked up at him wearing a crooked smile. Officer Riley wore the same crooked smile but for a different reason.

Riley said, only half under his breath, "I told you the butler did it. The butler always does it." He said this as he dialed 911 and summoned the paramedics to take the body away. After conferring with Pounce, Officer Riley cleared the room except for himself, the Police Commissioner, John Fulghum and Kim Su Baek.

While they waited for the emergency team to arrive, Pounce explained to the Commissioner, "In ancient Korea, particularly in the Joseon Dynasty, arsenic-sulfur compounds were used as a major ingredient of what was termed sayak, a poison cocktail used in capital punishment of high-profile political figures and members of the royal family. Due to social and political prominence of the condemned, many of these events were well-documented, often in the Annals of Joseon Dynasty. The former Korean executive assistant was from the Korean royal family, so she was well aware of this quaint tradition. Her family used it to good effect over the years. Just how much the Judge knew about poisoning, we'll probably never know."

Chapter 8

"When you turn away from seeing me
And go,
Though I die, no, not a single tear shall fall." — Kim Sowol,
Azaleas, trans. David R. McCann

After the successful séance in the Judge's study, Officers Pounce, Riley and Shaunessy returned triumphantly to the Boston Police Station. Bill Riley and Jim Shaunessy wanted to know whether the case of sayak had any precedence in the western tradition outside the notorious use of the substance by the Medici family in the Renaissance period.

Pounce sipped a cup of Dunkin' Donuts coffee and told them, "Theodor Gottlieb Ursinus, a high-ranking Prussian civil servant, and justice official, was poisoned by his wife Charlotte Ursinus in the year 1800. At the time, his death was ruled a stroke, but soon afterward, the widow was found to have poisoned, between 1797 and 1801, not only her husband, but also her aunt and her lover, as well as to have attempted to poison her servant in 1803. Her sensational trial led to the first reliable method of identifying arsenic poisoning."

The two young officers were agape at this knowledge.

"You can search the Net and discover everything about this. The same chemical analysis of the scentless, odorless substance was conducted locally to prove that the butler, who killed the others who had been poisoned, attempted to murder me and two others. The disadvantages of the murderer's demise are threefold. Justice is cheated of a criminal, we'll never know why the poisoner killed those people, and we've got to go back to our ordinary duties."

A week later Nigel and Molly Pounce dined with John Fulghum and Kim Su Baek at L'Espalier Restaurant in Boston. Miss Kim asked everyone to attend. She footed the bill.

Fulghum said, "Nigel, I've got to hand it to you. Your orchestration of the final act of the Anderson drama was masterful. Thank you for inviting me to the show."

Sue followed up. "I also want to thank you both for discovering the murderer of my father and mother and bringing him to justice. My parents would both be pleased if they were still with us."

"Sue, now that you've found your parents' murderers, what do you plan to do with the rest of your life?" Molly leaned forward to hear what the young woman would say.

"Mrs. Pounce, when I was in Seoul, I used to frequent a square reserved for penniless poets. I plan to return to my country and look in that square for a promising poet who will make a good husband."

Then she laughed. They all laughed heartily with her.

Pounce said, "We've solved a case, but I don't think we've come close to solving the real mystery." The policeman became pensive as he had broached a subject with no clear boundaries.

"Nigel is always venturing into the depths. He's done his job well, and we should be thankful." Molly was beaming with pride for her husband's success. "The Police Commissioner is recommending him for the highest medal awarded to active-duty officers."

"What do you think, John?" Pounce asked.

"Nigel, I think we should go fishing for the big one that got away. Ladies, there we were trolling for hours on the lake, with no bites except for mosquito bites. I think we weren't concentrating as much on fishing as on this case. The fish know when the fishermen are distracted. The answer is more fishing, but without the distraction."

Molly looked doubtful. Sue wrinkled her nose. Pounce, who understood his friend's irony and double entendres, raised his wine glass.

"Gunbae."

Everyone raised a glass and repeated the toast. They emptied their glasses for shortly after it was time for hugs all around and goodnights. Fulghum and Sue drove to the Boston Hilton where they had booked a suite for her last night in America. She wore her gold silk robe, and this time Fulghum wore monogrammed pajamas he had bought recently.

"John, why doesn't your monogram match your name?"

"Read it closely."

"Ah, so. I see it reads, 'JD.' For Jack Daniels. I should have known."

"Now that you know, please pour two glasses of the brown, velvety elixir of the gods. Since this is the last night I'm likely to share with you, don't you think you should level with me?"

"Whatever do you mean, John?" She looked up sideways from her concentration on her beautiful feet.

"What gives with the butler? Did you have any inkling he was the murderer? Even if you didn't, do you know why he was the murderer?"

"I can tell you only if you never repeat it to anyone else. I'll deny I said it. What do you say to that?"

"All right, Sue."   He raised his right hand. "I swear I won't tell what you're about to tell me to anyone for the rest of my life."

"All right. But you'll have to bear with me. This is complicated."

"Your complications are like my conditions. They go on and on. Remember you have a plane to catch tomorrow. Of course, we could delay your flight and extend our stay at this hotel. I'm ready to give you all the time you need."

"You're right. We have all the world and time, John, don't we? You have the codes for two accounts, each containing one million dollars. The third account is going to close because our arrangement is finished. After you submit your invoices, you'll be whole again and free of obligation to me."

He laughed. "So tell me what I want to know."

"Well, you know the butler did it. What I presume you want to know is why he did it, so I'll tell you what I think. While my father idolized my family, he also took care of many Koreans who came to America not to spy and kill but to find new lives. Some of those were good people with good intentions. Some of them were infiltrators of uncertain loyalties. In the case of our butler, we had no idea he was an agent of the DPRK, a breeding program product sent to infiltrate as a sleeper within our household."

"He looked Caucasian, not Asian. Are you convinced he was a product of the DPRK's breeding program?"

"I can't think of any other explanation. He was impeccably trained to act unlike an Asian. I think he was responsible for much more than the deaths of my mother and father. I do know he was waiting for a signal indicating he should execute my parents. He was clearly backed up by hit teams infiltrated by other means into the USA and by others not yet identified. Someone poisoned Mr. Frew, and I don't think the butler committed that murder."

"Why do you think he wanted to kill you, Pounce and me? We have clear and abundant evidence that he intended to do it in a very public way."

"I think he didn't have a will of his own. He was ordered to kill you by the current regime in North Korea. The current leader there Kim Jong-un is crazy. Everyone knows that. I suspect he was jealous of any arrangements he did not personally make. The deal cut between South Korea and my father went back to the time of Kim Jong-un's grandfather Kim Il Sung, whose intelligence staff infiltrated many DPRK agents including the butler."

"What about the lawyer and the writer who were killed? Were they killed on account of orders, or were they done as precautions against discovery of the long-term espionage plan of North Korea?"

"You must understand how a Korean thinks about these things. We are a people who like to control everything and everyone. As controllers, we want to eliminate any ambiguities."

"Why couldn't the KCIA have done everything you just described? Why are you so sure it was the DPRK?"

"KCIA officers are just not wired that way."

"Yet you admitted to me earlier that the three teams sent to kill were a mirror reflection of what the KCIA would have sent if they had the same aims."

"We Koreans are all one large family, John. How many times do I have to say it?"

Fulghum laughed and shook his head. "Are you really going back to find an impoverished poet as a husband in Korea?"

"I'd sincerely like that. Someone as strong and gentle as you are, John. I want someone genuinely patriotic in the right way, someone who'll help me make a difference."

"Are you afraid to go back after all you've been through?"

"Why should I be? John, I'm finally going home for good. I'm an educated woman desirous of starting a high-tech business."

"I don't think so," he flatly stated.

"Why not?" She asked, genuinely shocked he would disbelieve her.

"You're much too talented to waste your life adhering to performance ratios and herding sheep for the Korean version of Wall Street. Somehow, I can't visualize your being satisfied with a starving poet when you shoot like Annie Oakley and stand so cool under fire. Besides, I've known how you enjoy your sexuality and fine food. Are you going to find someone who can fulfill you as well as provide an anchor for your agility?"

"We'll see, John. I'm still young. I went online and discovered people can become Tennessee Squires. Do you think I could qualify? If so, will you help me apply?"

He laughed. Becoming a Tennessee Squire was a trivial matter once you were recommended by a current Squire in good standing. Fulghum's closest friends, like Nigel Pounce and Kenneth Mander, happened to be Tennessee Squires. They treated their status as if they formed a cabal of aficionados. An outsider like Sue naturally felt she might become one of Fulghum's inner circle by becoming a Tennessee Squire. Nothing could be further from the truth. Nonetheless, Fulghum decided to humor her.

"I can do that. Just give me a US address and email address and consider it done!"

"Who knows? We may meet again in the future."

"I'll never know what really passed between us, will I?"

"Why bother yourself with idle questions? Live for today! The rest is governed by things beyond our control."

That night Fulghum bade Sue farewell in the only way he knew. She seemed transported into ecstasy as he made love to her. She moaned and wept. She held onto him as if he were a life raft in a turbulent sea. Yet when she broke free from him, her sleep was sound and unperturbed. He could sense her withdrawal into her Korean self, a domain he could never invade or understand.

In the morning, he dropped Sue off at Logan International Airport with her suitcase and bag. As she climbed out of his car, she handed him a manila envelope containing a copy of the notebook with its decipherment as a parting gift. They walked about fifteen steps together then stopped and stood looking at each other, each trying to form a final image as a remembrance. Finally, she took the initiative and kissed him on the lips before she hurried off, waving goodbye over her shoulder. She continued waving as she went through the darkened glass doorway. Then she was gone.

As he walked back to retrieve his car, Ken Mander appeared suddenly beside him.

"How touching, John. You've seen your damsel off, and now you're right back where you started from. Do you care to spend a moment with me so we can both catch up?"

They segued in Fulghum's car to a far-removed area of the parking area where they shifted to Mander's vehicle. They sat there to review the bidding.

Mander opened the conversation with, "We found evidence the butler was a DPRK sleeper and a product of the breeding program. We can't connect all the dots, but we think Kim Su Baek was—and is—KCIA without ambiguity."

"I suppose that's why you let her live and return to her country."

"No comment. I also wanted to let you know we've cracked the code of the notebooks. I sure wish we'd received a copy of that notebook before Sue left."

Fulghum handed Mander the manila folder containing the copy and its decipherment.

"Don't say I never gave you something you actually wanted."

"If this is what I think it is, thank you, John. Of course, we'd like the other notebooks too, but beggars can't be choosers."

"Tell me about the Anderson estate as a long-term context for clandestine operations."

"The Agency allowed it as an enclave for the free transit of KCIA agents into and out of America. Anderson may not have been conscious of the fact, but he was working for us as much as for the KCIA. Along the way, the DPRK found the conduit attractive. They planned to infiltrate and potentially take over the estate. As for the timing of their move, the current leader is an impatient overreacher. He wanted to jump the gun before Anderson died a natural death. He wanted to take over the operational center right away."

"He failed."

"Perhaps at the Anderson estate he failed. The DPRK have had many other fish to fry."

"So the Anderson estate is not the North Koreans' only conduit."

"Nation-states, however small and cruel, have numerous accesses. They play to survive. We're looking into all such venues as Anderson controlled. That classified effort need not bother you."

"So what's left to do?"

"Darcy Figlear's royally pissed at you, John. Maybe you could invite her to your office for drinks and smokes?"

"Perhaps Silvia could help mollify her? Or Molly?"

"Speaking of Molly, I've arranged for Nigel to send her two dozen roses. She's the one who connected you to this grand enterprise. We wouldn't have arrived at a solution without your involvement. I wonder whether Nigel knows the treasure that he's married."

"You and I should be so lucky, Ken."

"In a way, we are that lucky. Your woman is a saint and an archivist. Mine is a saint and a bureaucrat. We may never sire heirs, but we'll have a great time making history with our significant others. Well, unless you have something else for me, I've gotta go."

"I'll see you, Ken, the next time. Until then, ciao."

They shook hands then Fulghum climbed out of the car and Mander drove off.

Fulghum felt alone and lonely when Mander's car disappeared. Instinctively, he checked his cell phone. On a hunch, he dialed Silvia's number. She picked up right away.

"Is the Korean bitch good and gone?"

"Yes, Silvia, she's gone. I'm at Logan now."

"And am I to be the sloppy seconds?"

"I just thought I'd call to see if you're all right."

"I'm fine. Thanks for asking. I'm also very thirsty."

"What do you say to my driving by to replenish your stock? What do you lack?"

"Only you, silly."

"Hold your thought. I'll be there in forty-five minutes, give or take. Will you forgive me?"

"Forgive what, you slob? Get your rear end over here and be safe doing it. I've got plans for us tonight."

"That gives me lots of ideas."

"It's about time. Oh, yes, your friend Jack Daniels is here to console me while you drive. He's quite the man."

"You have that right, my lady. Turn down the bed and pour us two to get us started."

Fulghum drove at the limit all the way to Silvia's pad. She met him at her apartment door with a glass of Jack Daniels whiskey in each hand. They fell into each other's arms and greeted each other warmly like the friends and lovers they had always been. Then she gave him one glass of the elixir and touched it with her own. They smiled and walked inside together.

Acronyms

AMTRAK -   Business name for American National Railroad Passenger Corporation

Arsenic and Old Lace – (1944) American dark comedy film directed by Frank Capra, starring Cary Grant, and based on Joseph Kesselring's play of the same name

CIA - Central Intelligence Agency

Ciao - Italian phrase for greeting or parting

CONUS - Continental United States

DDO - Deputy Director for Operations [of the CIA]

Demilitarized Zone - Area between North and South Korea established at the time of the Armistice that ended military conflict of the Korean War; aka DMZ

DPRK - Democratic People's Republic of Korea aka North Korea, to distinguish it from the Republic of Korea (ROK), which is termed South Korea

FBI - Federal Bureau of Investigation

Gunbae - a Korean toast equivalent to the English "Cheers!"

ID - Identification

JD - Jack Daniels whiskey

J.D. - Juris Doctor

KIA – Killed in Action

Korean War - The first military action of the Cold War. Active combat lasted from 1950 until 1953 and stopped with an armistice, but the war has never officially ended

Joseon - "The Great Joseon State" or Korean Kingdom founded by Yi Seonggye; it lasted for approximately five centuries, from July 1392 to October 1897

Judas goat - a trained goat that leads sheep to slaughter, while its own life is spared

KCIA - Korean Central Intelligence Agency

Kamsahamnida - Korean word meaning "Thank you."

Kim Sowol - Korean 'folk song poet' (1902-1934), author of Azaleas

Memento mori - Latin "reminder of mortality."

PC - Politically Correct

PI - Private Investigator

POWs - Prisoners of War

Pro bono - Latin phrase "for the public good"; legal, investigative or professional work undertaken at no charge

Sayak - Korean poison cocktail used in capital punishment of high-profile political figures and members of the royal family

USSR - Union of Soviet Socialist Republics aka The Soviet Union

E. W. Farnsworth

E. W. Farnsworth produces his work from his hometown in Arizona, USA. He has published a multitude of short stories, poems, and fiction both online and in print.

More than one-hundred-seventy short stories were published during 2014 through 2016, including many in Zimbell House Publishing, AudioArcadia.com, and Horrified Press anthologies. Some of Farnsworth's science fiction stories and modern fables are available online from Ether Books and Jotters United in the UK and fictuary.com in the US.

In 2015, *John Fulghum Mysteries* and *Engaging Rachel* were published by Zimbell House Publishing. Pro Se Productions published *Desert Sun, Red Blood*, a compilation of Arizonan western tales. *Bitcoin Fandango*, Farnsworth's picaresque novel about global intrigue in crypto-currency enforcement, appeared from Greenman Arizona Press.

During 2016, his writing created a collection of twenty-five visionary science-fiction stories available as *DarkFire at the Edge of Time* from AudioArcadia.com in England. In addition, his romantic collection, *Among Waterfowl & Other Entertainments*, plus his collected horror stories, *The Black Marble Griffon & Other Disturbing Tales* were published through Zimbell House Publishing; along with *Love in the Time of Baro Xaimos: A Novel of the Gypsy Holocaust* and *The Wiglaff Tales, Book One of the Wiglaff Chronicles*.

Forthcoming later in 2016 is his science fiction novel *Nightworld*, from AudioArcadia.com.

Stretching his writing talents even further, E. W. is currently working on an epic poem, *The Voyage of the Spaceship Arcturus*. A tale about the future of humankind when humans, avatars, and artificial intelligences must work together to manifest a second Eden after the Chaos Wars bring an end to life on Earth.

The next two installments of the John Fulghum Mysteries novels are contracted with Zimbell House Publishing for release in 2017.

Further information on the author can be found at the following URLs:

http://www.femalefirst.co.uk/books/e-w-farnsworth-desert-sun-red-blood-899035.html

http://www.zimbellhousepublishing.com/author-spotlight/e-w-farnsworth/

http://cindygrigg.com/2015/09/19/author-e-w-farnsworth-shares-his-inspiration-for-his-short-story-mobile-dusters-as-featured-in-psychopomps-shepherds-of-the-dead/

For continuous updates on the current and forthcoming works of E. W. Farnsworth, please see:

www.ewfarnsworth.com.

Reading Group Guide

1. John Fulghum has a mature, complex relationship with Silvia Blackwood. They are intellectual equals and partners, but their long-term affair is colored by events. Discuss the detective's relationships with Silvia and his client Sue as they reveal his attitudes towards women generally.

2. Judge Anderson is a complex, multifaceted character. How do you think his personality was shaped by his Korean War experience? Do you think all aspects of his life are explored in this novel? Why or why not?

3. The title of this novel contains symbolism and ambiguity. Explore the meaning of the color blue as it pertains to the origins of the Anderson family and the murders, and the attempted murders that are committed in the work. Whether in Boston or elsewhere, do you know the kind of people Fulghum briefly alludes to as the Lowells and the Cabots in his toast?

4. Officer Bill Riley's comment, "the butler always does it," seems comical in light of the literary tradition of the theme. Yet, in this case, the judge's butler, Albert Maynard, actually attempted to murder key figures, including Nigel Pounce, John Fulghum, and Kim Su Baek. Why do you think Maynard was a murderer? What was gained and lost by the butler's dramatic suicide? Who were the winners and losers from the butler's final act?

5. The relationship of John Fulghum and Nigel Pounce is close in both personal and professional ways. Discuss how their friendship helps solve the case of Judge Stephen Anderson's death. Do they share everything? Or do they keep some things secret from each other? Do you think their keeping secrets is a good thing?

6. Kim Su Baek is, on the one hand, a truly liberated woman. She is also a victim of her family's past. Discuss all you know about Sue as she is portrayed in this novel. What do her goals for her personal future suggest about her temperament and personality? Does she develop in the course of the novel, or is her character flat?

7. Why does Nigel Pounce assemble the specific people at the estate for his investigation? Does he know the outcome before he begins his proceedings? Did you guess what the outcome before it occurred?

8. Satire and irony are major devices in E. W. Farnsworth's fiction. Discuss how the novel gains resonance through irony of situation and other forms of irony. What kinds of things are satirized in the novel? Is Farnsworth criticizing New England life? The Boston Police Force? Justice in contemporary America? Other detective fiction?

9. In this novel, John Fulghum mentions the names of many other gumshoes to whom he refers mundane cases that do not interest him professionally. What is Fulghum's own perception of his role as a private investigator? Do you think the complicated nature of contemporary crimes requires his brand of detective work?

10. Fishing is just one metaphor that operates at a high level to inform the actions in this novel. Suggest how fishing relates to investigating. How do you think the metaphor of poisoning relates to Boston's blue blood society? Why was Judge Anderson known as a tiger in one instance and a rabbit in another?

A Note from the Publisher

Dear Reader,

Thank you for reading E. W. Farnsworth's third volume in the John Fulghum Mysteries series.

We feel the best way to show appreciation for an author is by leaving a review. You may do so on any of the following sites:

www.ZimbellHousePublishing.com
Goodreads.com
Amazon.com
or Kindle.com

Other Works by E. W. Farnsworth

John Fulghum Mysteries
John Fulghum Mysteries Vol. II
Engaging Rachel
Pirate Tales
Baro Xaimos: A Novel of the Gypsy Holocaust
Fairy Tales and Other Fanciful Short Stories
Among Water Fowl and Other Entertainments

The Black Marble Griffon & Other Disturbing Tales
The Wiglaff Tales: Book One of the Wiglaff Chronicles

Coming Soon from E. W. Farnsworth

John Fulghum Mysteries, Vol. IV: The Perfect Teacher

John Fulghum Mysteries, Vol. V: Finding Harry Diamond

Book Two of The Wiglaff Chronicles: The Emergence of the Shaman

9 781945 967368